THE FIN
ANGELS OR DEMONS

The Third Sonny Rider Novel

This is a work of fiction. Names, characters, organizations, places, acronyms, events and incidents are either the products of the author's imagination or are used fictitiously.

Copyright © 2018 Sonny Rider

All rights reserved.

No part of this book may be reproduced, or stored in a retrieval system, or transmitted in any form or by any means or otherwise without express written permission.

Cover Image: The Lakeview Cemetery, Columbus, Ohio; The Haserot Angel of Death Victorious. Her bronze, weather, and age result in the visible tears. Her weapon wielding is to conquer death – until then she waits and weeps. It was created for the Haserot family by Herman Matzen. The author would like to thank the groundskeeper too.

First Edition

The author would like to acknowledge the wonderful people that make up the South Western Oregon Coast. Their courage is only surpassed by their kindness, and recognition of U.S. Veterans. From Bandon to Coos Bay and North Bend – all the way to Florence; these towns are adding tourism and seafood to the many splendors of Oregon. These robust communities also provide some of the largest amount of timber to the world. All of the above under the protection of the local U.S. Coast Guard, and their life-flight helicopter crew. As a proud naval tradition, "Fair Winds, and Following Seas."

My very dear thanks to the small ranch and timber community of Seneca, Oregon it is a refuge and center for forest fire response and lookouts. The people are welcoming and continue to be the author's favorite neck of the woods, (Murders Creek).

This book is dedicated to my family, they have continued to support the drive within me to write, and to my wife Barbara; she has plowed through adversities, to allow me to still read my stories to her. Thanks to my fans that still follow my work today!

PROLOGUE

Paul was no angel. He was a simple man in an earthly world of corruption, corporate bailouts, and a dog-eat-dog political system. Living in a small town in Oregon, he found Coos Bay to be a spot that suited him.

There were times in his life when Paul was held captive, and wished secretly, that he was dead. It would have been a welcome torment end – no one would ever have blamed him. On the contrary, most would wonder why he hadn't taken his own life a long time ago, if they knew the torture and torment that Paul had known. Paul knew the media would make a circus of his death, in the manner which they would spin the truth hard enough to sell anything. Paul often wondered if the President were to cure cancer, the headlines of some news media would read, "After decades of wealth, and billions spent, finally a result is maybe possible." It probably would paint a bleak picture of Paul as well, even though he had done so much for others. The love and healing of so very many people by Paul would be forgotten, long enough for him to be damned.

Some educated fool from a national media newscast would point out that Paul was helping someone in a location; when he should have been somewhere else to help someone that may be linked to the newscaster. It was *amazingly* easy to blame anyone for something. While the Hindu people found peace, tranquility, and Paul's healing ability to be a gift; the Catholic Church was challenging the validity of miracles that Paul performed. There was no way of avoiding conflict in everything Paul was trying to do in a sinful world, determined upon destruction. The irony that Paul was aware of, (that seem to escape everyone else) was that Paul was only given the gift of healing by God for a specific number of uses. The number was rising fast; as Paul was dying slowly, gradually; each and every time he had healed someone.

He knew what the bible had made references to, "Be not deceived; God is not mocked: for whatsoever a man soweth, that shall he also reap." Paul had tried hard to sow love and kindness, beating down the hate that had been spreading throughout the country. The sixteen-year, young, black teen from a Chicago Black Gangster Disciples, that was shot by a policeman, that Paul healed; resulting in him hugging Paul and tossing his colors away. The gang was speechless, when the teen apologized to the very policeman that had taken his life only minutes before.

Paul had accomplished unity so very much, by doing exactly what God had told him to do…or was it Buddha, or Muhammad, or maybe Jehovah…he didn't know or care. Even when Paul was finally in his fifties and all those miners of West Virginia that were found dead all lined up like cord wood; that Paul's prayer and touch had brought them back to life, were greeted by tears, and by believing, loved ones. The media, of course, attributed it to the CPR that had failed by First Responders. The little girl in Wisconsin that had fallen through the ice, Paul had brought her from a faded blue, to the pink and crying toddler grappling for her mother. That one rang so warmly in Paul's memory; he felt as though he had done so very much; but it was now just another canyon in the shadows of his memory.

It all seemed a bit incredible at the time, a media circus, a national calling of halting the violence, the damning of hate crimes; Paul just wanted to show the power of **love** over hate. It seemed like the thing that he most wanted in life, so he pursued it vigorously. But it had obviously taken its toll on him. He knew from his brother Lance, that an Angel burns twice as bright; but for only half as long. It was a matter of life – and death. It took Paul back to the beginning, and how this whole crazy nightmare started, when he was just simply, Paul. Before all the pomp and circumstance, before the fame, before the lure of money or power, before he found the gift from God; before he knew the battle with darkness. When he was just a man in an earthly world – that knew nothing of "*The Healing*".

The Finding of Angels and Demons

Chapter 1

Paul Baldwin used to live in Nebraska, but due to situations that were out of control; his entire family moved to Oregon. They lived in the mountains of Eastern Oregon for quite some time, but then as he grew older, Paul longed for the water and the coast of Oregon. This ultimately had led him to the small, but growing community of North Bend, and Coos Bay. It was almost impossible to mention one without the other, it was like so many small towns throughout America. One small community would envelope another, and finally a single sign that most people miss, separated the two towns. In a blink, a driver would be in one town, and a second later, quite another town. Paul remembered the same situation in Eastern Oregon. He would drive to Canyon City, and a second later, he was in John Day, Oregon. Typically, through history, most towns have leadership that will make sacrifices to meet, converge, and unite money and resources to conglomerate into a single city. But…there are always the hold – outs, the determined few, the proud.

In this case, the local high school mascots, and teams of sports in their school; were rivals. Coos Bay loved their teams as much as North Bend loved their teams. Since the two communities were both around 10k in population, they played hard to defeat each other, (and any other takers out there!) The Reedsport rivalry was the only thing that helped support the old saying, "The enemy of my enemy, is my friend" so there was a shred of dignity and respect between Coos Bay and North Bend. While it was fragile, but existent in the schools, it was a bit more complicated when it came to politics or real estate.

The secret that no one discussed; or at least it was a bit of an elephant in every room – was that both Coos Bay and North Bend had enveloped other communities that continue to use their old regional names. Paul would be invited to watch a football game at someone's house, the address would undoubtedly conclude with "Empire" as the address. Empire was a small district or region that connected North Bend with the nearby town of Charleston. Maybe the oral address given, would include Marshfield, or Glasgow, or Eastside, or Englewood, or something else. It was incredible, if someone was raised in the area, they all knew exactly where these areas were, good luck to any tourist. Paul would laugh at someone on a GPS that would navigate electronically. They were destined to be led astray and they may land in Hauser, or even up at a prison!

Paul was only now figuring out that if you told someone local that you lived in Coos Bay, they would always follow up with asking where. It was almost a sure sign that you were a tourist, (staying with family) or you were fresh to the neighborhood and bought blindly. It could be argued that everyone that moved to the Oregon Coast was moving blindly. There was this Cascadia Faultline that would undoubtedly shift and cause a very serious earthquake and/or tsunami to rein down hell on folks. Paul didn't seem to think that he would live in fear, and he loved the climate of constant fifties and sixties for temperatures. It rained in the winter, but after below freezing temperatures and piles of snow in the mountains, Paul found the coast climate refreshing.

The seafood was great, the people seemed to genuinely honor Veterans, (as their county entry signs proudly reflected.) There was a bit of an older – sixties, retirement community with the plethora of doctors, hospitals, and the lawyers that follow. The entire huge cargo ships that load raw logs in the inlet is hard to mistake. These mammoths would pull in and consume long stacks of millions of board feet of timber. They would then depart for whereabouts unknown, their crew hoping for mild seas. The small Oregon bay was perfect in its infancy stage, when tree barons would ship the timber via the port. It was now industrialized, but the local forest protection agencies did great work to plant trees, trap boomers, and protect against fire. Timber has always been king in Oregon. Combined with fishing and hunting; Paul was just fine enjoying his first job out of college.

Paul was a trained and licensed Veterinarian. As a youngster, Paul wanted to help small animals. If he could set them to healing, he was excited and joyous. He had watched an old film when he was a kid, it was called *"Thomasina"* and it was a story of a Veterinarian and a woman that was perceived as a witch, the story unfolds to bring the two together via tragedy. After the thirteenth time of watching it as a kid, his mother had sadly advised the tape was eaten and could no longer play. Paul was heartbroken, Mom was mysterious, and Paul's brothers were celebratory. It was okay, because Paul bought a DVD later!

Paul had lots of entertaining DVD's about humor, animals, and even home videos that had animals for content. He grew up with pets, his first cat was a mongrel mix, as was the dogs, ferret, guinea pig, and that Vietnamese Potbelly Pig, (named Porky.) Paul once tried to utilize a nine-volt battery to resuscitate a white rat, (that his mother was glad did not regain consciousness!) But there were far more success stories, the mending of a broken wing of a bird, (that learned to say, "Oh my toe!" while in captivity.) There was that time that a flying squirrel that his dad had brought home in a lunch box to release in the living room! That flying rodent was going to be killed by his mother if someone didn't catch it and avoid it's claws and teeth, to remove it to the outdoors from flying around the living room draperies.

Paul was courageous when the situation called for it, he used the drapery to catch it, and shake it off outside. Genius was the word he used to describe himself after performing the magic trick with the flying squirrel. The squirrel wasn't really the source of the anger, Uncle Tuffy had given the boys battery powered flying helicopters that loved to entangle and rip into a new hairdo... "ouch" was the only word that was not a cussing jar offense on that occasion. Paul found that he was torn as a teenager, he loved to hunt deer and elk, but his love in life was healing animals. It was something that he was so confused about that he asked his father about it. His father simply explained that God placed animals on the earth for man to rule over – but he reminded Paul, "You may judge the character of a man or woman by how they treat animals."

Paul had found there were no bad dogs, just bad owners. But for the people that couldn't afford to help or heal their animal, Paul would always step in, and reduce the expense of anything he could do personally. As a result, he often had to euthanize pets for free, or skip charges that would help the clinic ultimately. It seemed like the right thing to do, so Paul figured, maybe it's a karma thing that could finally catch up one of these days. Paul didn't mind laughing at himself, he would often make some clumsy mistake in front of customers, like trip or get bitten, he would then yell, "Live from New York – it's Saturday Night!" He had found that anytime he did something clumsy, the phrase seemed to bail him out with laughter from a crowd or group. There were plenty of strange Vet calls, and a strange pet now and then that would come into and leave Paul's care. Just like any other profession, there were always a few surprises that occur.

Paul was called once to a discreet location, because a red-tailed hawk had swooped into an office space and was perched on the cubicle. Not threatening anyone, but eyes that followed every movement, (including the use of the phone for help.) Now and then, he would need to get his marksman tranquillizer dart rifle, when bear, cougar, or some other odd thing needed taken to safety. Paul especially laughed out loud on the way back from a call once, regarding a pet cat needing rescued. When he arrived at the residence, the door was open, but the screen door allowed the woman to communicate the request to come in. When Paul found the semi-nude woman in a leopard leotard laying on the couch purring; he asked where the cat was, the only reply was a finger pointing at her own anatomy. Paul thanked her and advised her there would be no charge for the home visit, and she would be placed on the "Do Not Call List".

It wasn't like he wasn't tempted, but how would he tell his mother how they met, and she probably had twenty years on him too. It wasn't something that would bring honor to him or the clinic. He laughed on the way home, thinking of how he would inaccurately describe how he handled the call to the folks at the office. No, he probably would simply ignore the thing and it would go away, and so it did. Paul wasn't a gambler, but since there were two casinos in the town, it was tolerated, and often avoided. Once he received a call that there was a Personal Service Dog incident at one of the two casinos. He responded to find a small dog that was wearing a personally crocheted vest that stated, "Service Dog" on it. It apparently was to help the owner combat the addiction of gambling…at the casino. The man had lost, the dog was kicked, and the casino security called the local Police, who then called Paul. Sometimes it was tough to fathom who the beasts were.

The strangest call could have been the Californian that caught a fish, put it in the live well hold, then when he got back, had second thoughts; rushed the fish to Paul to save. Paul promptly advised the well-dressed fisherman, that he would not be able to save it, but would take care of the tuna for the man. It was so delicious on the barbeque at work the next day, the office folks had a party.

Paul was just simply getting started in his life when the illness took about eighty pounds of weight off him. After the chemo, he just wanted to die, but he was hopeful and optimistic as everyone in that position. He was flown to a University Hospital in Portland, which was ready to carry out clinical trials of a new drug that had shown some promise. Paul agreed in writing and the two-week duration of treatment almost killed him. Looking back, Paul wondered if that wouldn't have been better. It took almost six months for him to completely get enough health back into his body to try and come back to work. He finally recovered and was blessed to hear his doctor advise him to begin cutting back on all medication and to simply, eat healthy again. It was a great relief to him and his family.

Something had happened that cluttered the news channels when Paul got home that day from work and his return party. When he changed channels, it was the same story that continued to be re-hashed. Apparently, there was some accident involving several bee Colony Collapse Disorder events in the Middle East, but it had something to do with birds as well. The World Health organizations, and United Nations were calling upon assistance from Ornithologists, Melittologists, (a branch of entomology studying bees) and they were requesting Veterinarians to report any unusual behavior to Homeland Security via a website and phone number.

Scientists hadn't done enough work on bird-spreading Avian Influenza; but it made sense that birds do migrate, and they cover the world. No one seemed to be doing any research on the connectivity of birds and bees, (other than the sexual connotation.) There were only one-thousand cases of "bird flu" in the US each year. But then the unusual combination of whatever the bees carried, that were consumed by birds – resulted in a unique, more deadly effect on people.

Bird Flu, (also referred to as H5N1) spreads by airborne droplets, and usually requires a medical diagnosis. Lab tests or imaging is often required, and there was the issue that this year, the strain was unique. Obviously the more unique, the more difficult to battle; and time is always a factor. The timing of flights, wind, moisture, and the specific strain – having time to infect. As the media circus began to grow, it should have been isolated, tracked, battled, and dedicated professionals/money thrown at it early. But it was too little, too late.

Paul had received a request for assistance from the local Coast Guard in Coos Bay. It wasn't too much of a surprise, he helped them in the rescue of pets often. The contact between Paul and the USCG usually involved marine life. This time, it was a bit unique, it was a request to fly out to a large cruise ship, to provide assistance to pets aboard the vessel.

Apparently, they were prepared to pay handsomely, and he would be helicoptered by the USCG in one of the orange birds he saw regularly. It sounded like fun, so Paul agreed to assist. The briefing before the flight was a bit loud; the rotors were turning, the pilot was talking, and Paul was thinking…but none seemed in concert. Instead it seemed like a desperate effort to please everyone, so Paul stepped aboard the aircraft and someone helped buckle him into the "star" looking multiple strapped safety harness.

Once airborne, Paul could appreciate the view of the bay rather quickly, (making notes of several areas that he knew locally.) The windspeed was steady, the pilot compensated rather quickly, and they were headed west and out to the Pacific Ocean quickly. It was a couple hours later that a small speck on the horizon soon became visible to Paul as a large cruise ship. It got a heck of a lot larger, as he grew closer, preparing to land on the tail heliport. As the large craft didn't dive and buck in the ocean, the waves only slightly tilted it a little back and forth in a steady rhythm. It almost made Paul sleepy watching the comfort of the motion, as they set down lightly on deck.

An officer of the crew approached and met Paul as he disembarked the aircraft. The guy was talking to Paul, but he still couldn't hear, as the blades whirred-up and took the pilot back to his destination. Finally, Paul entered via a door-like hatch, and he shook hands with Kevin. They shared some info, and Kevin asked Paul to accompany him as they continued to walk through the maze of passageways that were bustling with tourists. Paul and Kevin finally got to the Ship Infirmary and medical facility. It seemed modern, there was a plethora of medication behind a secured, gated, pharmacy. Next was a couple cubicles that were dedicated to dentistry, and each had the water, drills, and gadgets that Paul disliked so very much.

Next on the tour was a room with the X-Ray and some lead aprons hanging on the wall for use. The treatment area was adjoining a small waiting room that probably could handle a dozen people. There was a water fountain for taking meds and lots of reading material available. In the very back of the treatment area, there was a reverse-pressure room, that was equipped to isolate any airborne pathogen, (like Tuberculosis) pulling in filtered air and piping it up to the safety of the highest levels to exhaust.

Kevin thanked Paul for coming, advising that he had other duties to attend to and he gave him a card that had phone numbers to key locations on the ship. Kevin advised Paul, the ship doctor would be joining him as his personal guest, to answer any further questions and show him to his room later. Paul thanked him, and Kevin departed, leaving Paul to explore. Paul found a closet door at the back of the room near a coat hanger. He hung his coat and then opened the closet, only to find there were about six or seven birds in cages that were definitely ill or dead.

As the doctor entered the room, he exclaimed, "You should close that door, I may have to isolate those birds in the reverse-pressure room next!" Dr. Clint Johnson introduced himself as Paul closed the door quickly.

"This is the weirdest thing I've ever seen," Dr. Johnson began, "these are all pet birds accompanying the guests aboard the vessel. They are in distress or dying, and I can't stop it. I'm only now finding the owners of the pets are now having medical problems. I am not sure if it's connected, but I need a vet to examine these birds and isolate them for examination upon our next port of call."

Paul was cleaning his hands after touching the door latch and other items, he then dried his hands and shook hands with the doctor. "Look," he stated firmly, "I'm no doctor, but I strongly recommend that we begin isolating the impacted passengers in this reverse pressure, isolation chamber immediately," Paul advised. "Even if it's for only a few days, you should be able to tell more by then," Paul reasoned.

"These passengers paid money for a cruise," the doctor excused, "it takes a definite order for me to isolate and justify to the Captain that we need to quarantine people or have an epidemic response!" The doctor seemed to be squeamish about taking any action, he didn't want to upset anyone, Paul thought he probably was what he referred to as "RIP" or "Retired in Place" and wouldn't do anything to exercise his ability. Paul asked to see his quarters, to throw his bag, and personal hygiene items. He was given a map and shown where to find his quarters. The doctor seemed too busy to deal with the urgent issue, and Paul advised he would get into protective clothing, and examine the birds immediately upon returning from his quarters. A deckhand showed him to his quarters, and he was surprised to see there was very nice accommodations. Paul turned his map upside down to reverse his course from his room to get back to medical.

Although the seas were calm, the storm about to hit the ship; was of a different nature. Paul was busy within the infirmary sorting equipment to protect himself upon entering the bird room. He identified several types of mask available but decided to go with an SCBA to ensure he was only breathing oxygen. He then donned a full protective suit and proceeded to take equipment into the room. Just as he was about to enter, the phone rang. He knew that he could not speak on the phone, due to the suit and the seal, but his instinct made him pick up the phone. It was the doctor advising him not to enter the bird room.

The doctor was yelling something about the pet owners had went to dinner, and all hell was breaking loose. Apparently, the epidemic that spread even more quickly than anyone could have expected. Food had been taken to various decks and even to the bridge, people were vomiting profusely over the deck railings and on to other people puking below. The ship's sewer systems were failing, and potable water they found, would become scarce quickly. The doctor requested Paul to remain in the infirmary, while he dealt with the chaos below. Paul knew it could be the last time he might speak to the doctor, but the suit prevented it. As he hung up the phone, Paul grabbed some essential inhalers, water, and some MRE's that he found. He left the suit on and took the provisions into the reverse pressure chamber.

Paul found that the chamber was equipped with a small television. He quickly turned it on and whisked through the channels to find the ship's CCTV. There was a banner running across the top advising all passengers returned to their quarters and await instructions. Most passengers and crew believed it was food poisoning. Paul could feel the ship turning sharply, probably heading directly for port. Paul imagined the cruise company would be refunding or giving vouchers to any of the survivors. It was still unclear how many people could survive, or if it would even be fatal. Paul felt safe in the chamber with the suit on. Over the next hour, Paul would surf the TV channels available to see similar chaos evolving on the shore.

Hospitals were being overrun, the outbreak was spreading quicker than ever imagined; it was like something out of the Hitchcock thriller, but in apocalyptic proportions. FEMA would only take a stab at it, Homeland Security would only try to find blame, and medical resources would be completely wiped out before the ship Paul was on would come to port. It was apparent to Paul, that he would be returning to world different than that he had left. He began to worry about family, friends, the office, and even pets. Like a sledgehammer, the reality hit him - what would the world be like without birds? He then felt guilty for being inside the suit and chamber. He flashed back to the CCTV channel to see the anticipated arrival time to arrive back in port. The ship was running at full speed back to an unknown, but in an hour and a half - somebody better put on the brakes. Paul was thinking that he would time the ship's arrival, and just before it hit shallow water, he would jump. He believed the protective suit would mitigate the fall. But then he wondered what he would do in the world all alone, what if this wiped out civilization and there were no survivors? It seemed unfair that he had battled illness so vigorously, taken all the drugs, and just got back to a normal working life; only to survive an epidemic that may kill everyone else.

    Paul finally decided that he would take off the suit when the oxygen bell rang, and then he would take equipment and resources from the infirmary to the people who needed it below. Damned if he would hide out this Armageddon, epidemic, plague, or bird flu - he would meet it head on, provide assistance to those in need. The bell rang early, making Paul jump with nervousness. He took off the protective headdress, disrobed from the suit, and then slipped off the SCBA. He paused for a moment before he opened the door, asking himself if this was the right decision. He laughed to himself as he opened the door, grabbed some supplies and exited the chamber. He then grabbed some yellow caution tape and cross the bird room door with it. Hoping that it would restrict anyone from going in, all though it probably wouldn't matter.

    Taking the supplies, Paul headed out with his trusty color-coded map of the ship. Paul had forgotten that he would be showing symptoms like everyone else; he was only focusing on helping other people. Within about five minutes, he exited an external door to the deck that was open before him. He expected to see bodies stacked like cordwood, but he was surprised to see organized groups of people bivouac and sorted by degree of illness. The doctor was periodically puking into a piña colada glass, providing treatment, emptying the glass overboard, and then returning to provide more treatment. Whatever the doctor was doing, it seemed to be working. Passengers were exiting their rooms in anticipation of the ship's arrival in port. All of them appeared seasick, nauseous, there didn't seem to be any fatalities. Paul offered his services to the doctor and began hoping where he could. Apparently, the navigator and the captain were on the bridge preparing to bring the vessel into port. The entire fiasco turned out to be nonfatal, and treatment was identical to that of the flu. Paul laughed to himself when he considered telling his tale when he got back to the office, admitting his fear and placed him in the chamber in the suit. The girls would get a laugh out of that, he thought to himself.

To say that this would be quite a story to add to his veterinarian collection, would be an understatement; but it still worried him that the speed of the epidemic, however slight, was lightning quick. No one had ever seen the speed of the illness in the history of modern medicine. The major news media would be unsure of how to report it, and the disease control centers would be unsure of how to combat it. Paul didn't even notice that he was exhibiting no symptoms as the ship prepared to pull into port. Although Coos Bay was not the intended location for the cruise ship to arrive, the port master cleared them with the Coast Guard escort, and they proceed slowly. Paul looked down, identifying the location that he would have jumped, that he now had aborted. Glad that he didn't have to jump, he smiled as if he was the only one to get the joke. No one on the ship, would know what to expect upon the arrival.

It was a bleak and dismal day by weather standards, but with the epidemic looming over everyone's head, it would truly be one of the worst days of their lives. The large ship seemed a lot smaller when at sea, as it slowly entered it appeared much bigger. The Coast Guard Cutter guided the ship safely to the designated area that it was prepared for the gangplank once tied off. There were several ambulances and law enforcement present in preparation to receive the ship. Paul was like everyone else, they all just wanted off the ship as quickly as possible. Hundreds of people clambered, some of the passengers could have won Emmy awards as it appeared their injuries were now tenfold. It was apparent that there were not enough wheelchairs, so Paul contacted his office and had two more delivered. The local TV news media was on hand, but the show was all too familiar because the epidemic struck landfall as well already.

Paul was anxious to find out about friends and family, so we didn't even notice that he still was not exhibiting any symptoms. As he poured into the funnel of people all wanting to get off the ship as quick as possible he found the anxiety overwhelming, he could not imagine if the epidemic would have been fatal. The people pouring out the ship reminded him of cattle, they had lost their decency somewhere or at least their temperament hours ago. Normally, the ship coming into port that was not scheduled with the complications that the ship had would've been huge news, but the small town was still reeling from the impact of the epidemic and people were still freaked out.

Most of the emergency equipment in town had been bought or looted; the usual items that could not be found were batteries, water, fresh food, and some key medications. The various shelters in the area had been stacked to overpopulation capacity. The hospitals found themselves overwhelmed, and the small community supported multiple doctors and nurses for the local retirement communities, found themselves to be rare commodities. Some of the elderly had not survived, so it would be unfair to say that the epidemic was not fatal. The death rates throughout the state and nation were moderately low, considering the speed which the epidemic traveled. Always the young and elderly impacted the most, Paul was surprised to find animals not affected. It would take several months study and tests to understand the full impact of the epidemic.

When Paul finally got home, he found answers on his phone recorded, a small stack of mail, and several notes from work tacked to the door. Jumping in the shower, he wanted to wash away the memories what he'd seen and what he had experienced like dirt washed down the shower drain. He spent an extra 10 minutes in the shower just letting the water massage his hair and head. When he turned the water off, his entire body seemed disappointed to end the shower. He shook his head and grabbed a towel drying off quickly. He couldn't stop thinking about the bizarre, lightning speed at which the medical condition that had spread, impacted, and then diminished when treated promptly. Paul knew he was no doctor, but as a veterinarian if he were treating animals effected, he would try to isolate them to figure out how to treat and study the disease.

It seemed to be the only thing that people watched on the news, and since it had happened on the shore already, Paul saw no reason to tell his story to the office crew. As Paul would go to work, he would see the public wearing the worthless masks after the fact. He supposed that if it made them feel safe, the placebo mask would be seen around town for months. There was the very best the country had to offer, working on the problem, and apparently it had become an international issue. Americans would watch on television the impact of the epidemic on other countries. It was so very sad to see the poor undeveloped countries finding the epidemic to be fatal. Paul seemed hypervigilant about the world health after surviving his treatment the year before. It seemed after work each day, he would watch the news on the television as they would hypothesize on what caused or cured, seem to elude the world medical professionals. Paul continued to monitor his health, but never noticed any symptoms. He felt better than ever before; watching so many on television that were ill, made Paul feel guilty for feeling so well.

As the months followed; most of the people infected received treatment as soon as it was available resulting in lowered fatalities. Some scientists believed there may be residual effects that they would continue to study. Everyone he knew including family and friends, coworkers, and pet owners had been infected and survived. It was the buzz on social media, famous people were describing their own personal survival of the epidemic. It seemed that everyone had their own heroic tale to tell. Paul never told anyone his tale, it didn't seem that important. Soon there were other impactful events is in the world that seem to take the spotlight, and the public's focus on the epidemic dimmed. Paul seemed to have forgotten that he never was ill. If he would have thought of it, the timing of his previous treatment combined with the hazmat suit inside the reverse chamber; would probably be the scientific answer for why he was never impacted. Whatever the reason may be, Paul had not become infected.

Paul religiously phoned home to his family every two weeks, his family was proud of him. Sometimes he would call his parents and other times, they would call him when necessary. Keeping in touch with family was important to him, but he found it difficult at times just like everyone else. When he finally got a hold of his mother, Paul seemed to ask more questions than providing answers. He was just as worried about his family as they were of him. Paul found out that they too, had been impacted by the epidemic. It was a relief to mothers across the nation to have found the epidemic was not fatal. Paul neglected to tell his family he was not affected, it just never came up. It probably would've been difficult for Paul to explain why he wasn't affected and the circumstances surrounding it. In reflection, it probably would have been a great relief for Paul to have told his mother he was not impacted.

The secret of Paul not being infected, would be his to keep alone. He was not a proud man, even though his family was proud of him. He would not boast, he wasn't even sure if he was worthy of the gift, for showing what he believed was cowardice. He did not want this single weakness to bend, alter, or even impact the future. Regretfully, it was this catalyst that seemingly changed his life. Perfect timing of a lifetime event, colliding with a situational access to the perfect equipment – had equaled a perfect storm of protection. It would be several months before Paul would begin to realize something that was truly miraculous, a revelation that would have defied medical science, and set the modern world back on its heels!

The revelation was simple, God interjects and protects people when they don't even realize it, showering down individual blessings, specific to each person at the perfect time, when it matters most. Paul would pray, just as the rest of the world would, and some answers to prayer would be apparent – but an endless bounty of protection and love would be **unseen and anonymous**; as intended. Hospitals generated prayers, mortuaries generated prayers, cemeteries generated prayers - churches, mosques, temples, synagogues, even dates, generated prayers. Paul was about to find out that; these numerous examples combined, were only a *sliver* of the protection and love that was anonymous. Apparently, the numerous blessings were anonymous, because they were delivered by angels on earth from the heavens above.

Chapter 2

Paul didn't claim to know or understand God, and he didn't care what name the people of the world used. He did know that his brother Lance had served in some honorable society of Knights that had religious foundations, and his parents brought him up – God fearing and loving. He knew in his heart to do the right thing, although sometimes he wasn't sure if he could pin that tricky thing down. Just as Taoists believed in the Ying and Yang, Christians believed in blessings and sin; there was a struggle in the universe that centered around this crazy big planet, Earth. Since the beginning of time, or Cain and Abel; it really didn't matter what your ethnicity was, your color, or even what language you spoke – people were behaving either good – or bad.

There were far too many things that Paul didn't know, but since the accident at sea, blessing at sea, or coincidence/timing; he found himself not knowing a hell of a lot more! Questions would hit him a lot harder, curiosity would tempt him more, and over the next ten years…Paul would have to act without knowing some answers, blindly trying to focus!

The future was always clouded, but things were about to happen to the young vet that would question his own values, and ability to judge people. He had returned to a home that had been shattered and scarred by epidemic, the nation had been turned upside down. The pointers in the media were quick to stick out their judgmental hand and try to place blame. You could blame the government for not being prepared; you could always blame them for anything and everything. Political affiliations blamed each other, because it's what they did…someone should have butchered that damn donkey and elephant and feasted on anything but crow! Some political hardliners would be screaming rhetoric up to the point that they died. Paul believed that heaven would not care which party you are affiliated with at that point.

In a land of millions of pharmacies, restrictions, FDA, and abuse; there would be no pill to pop to avoid or dodge this epidemic. No…this puppy was impacting every nation around the globe. Guerillas fighting in Honduras, Rangers fighting terrorism in Afghanistan, and even the starving that were fighting for food in Kenya – everyone that was too old or too frail were lost to the epidemic. For every one that did die, there were two or three in hospitals that could afford the care to try and survive this celestial sweeping of the globe. For some odd reason, or slip of someone's tongue, the epidemic was finally titled by a society nickname, "Birdfire".

Paul thought that because of the manner in which the epidemic was spread, via the avian feathers of fate; that someone associated it with birds. The fire was the effects on the body afterward; fever, vomiting, and chills were typical. Many did survive this Armageddon of influenza, but it hospitalized them due to other complications, (some previous health issues). One thing was certain, the hospitals were overwhelmed with the populous. The result was a typical outcome that everyone should have expected; instead of being shocked. The hospitals began to triage, taking those with health insurance, and staging appointments for everyone that couldn't afford or didn't have health care. Insurance companies were scrambling to re-word policies to include an, "Act of God" to avoid bankruptcy and to pay huge.

The stock market tumbled as did the brokers from the top of buildings. Investors circled, not knowing where to invest, deciding on grasping for all they could before it was lost; or found unimportant now. The chaos of city violence, looting, and all the badness that went with it; found most of the world reeling in fear. Guns were coveted, hidden and sold in the black market. Ammo was scarce, and reloading became heavenly training that was hard to find or hold on to. Most large predatory animals or flying predators moved up on the evolutionary ladder. There were issues of animals attacking humans because they were scared, scarred, or starving. Paul found several times that upon reporting to assist, when pets aren't fed or cared for, they tend to scavenge…if the pet owner was frail or fell, it became possible food. Dogs and cats would be found guilty numerous times by people, when the animal was the victim too.

In any case, Paul didn't like the animals being ordered to be euthanized, but he was often ordered by the local authority. He would usually intervene if he could, but sometimes he would find a "win – win" situation, by simply darting them to sleep, then hauling them elsewhere that they could survive, and turning them loose. He didn't track if they came back into societal focus or simply disappeared to a quiet and solitary life elsewhere.

Animals were always second to people however, Paul had intervened several times in his life, that saved both people and pets. But he simply would dismiss it, because that's what people do, he figured. He never was a front-stage fellow; Paul was a social introvert, he often found it more tolerable to trust animals, than people. Animals, when hurt will lash-out and hurt you, but like a rattlesnake, there are warning signs to every animal. People, on the other hand; tend to stick to "fight or flight" in a conflict or crisis. Most folks run away from a dangerous situation, (it's probably proving Darwin's theory of survival). But some, mostly health care officials, law enforcement, (Correction included) will run toward the situation in an attempt to respond or save lives.

Paul simply had found a lot of falsehood in people, they often could exemplify one of the alleged "seven deadly sins" and this can be really deceitful, when combinations occur in folks' behavior. Paul had met and seen some angelic type folks too, that would lay down their life for you. Paul believed that his brothers were perhaps those that fell into the latter group. Paul certainly would try to save someone if he could, (even if grabbing them could involve pulling him to his death too.) But what Paul could never figure on, was the unaccounted, unpredictable, and unforeseen elements in peoples' soul. Any man or woman would reach out to grab a rope to save their life, some might even give up their seat on a lifeboat, but there are a few "Titanic men" that would slither into a lifeboat when women and children were being called!

To be able to assess a man's soul, to feel his integrity, to test his character, and find if he has *"True Grit"*; would be great; to pick the next person for that seat in the lifeboat. But regretfully, there was no such tool, (the right pick would be found three decks down…helping others to escape!) Many would say a Psychiatrist, Psychologist, or Sociologist could be a good judge of character, maybe even a Criminologist would be able to be most accurate. Regretfully, they all left on earlier lifeboats.

Paul never imagined that he would be the person that would have to judge men, women, and children to determine who may be worthy of saving. It would be a task that he would love to have gaffed-off and shoved to someone more fitting or suited to perform this challenge. But it was forced upon him, he would have to learn the ropes quickly, muddle through the best he could, and maybe even make some good judgement calls. There was no school for judging character; Paul would have to learn with his feet running as he hit the ground. His greatest fear was probably in his mind battling the theory that "absolute power – corrupts absolutely".

It would never do to let power consume him; Paul would be humble, modest, caring, and do the right thing; because it was the right thing to do! He convinced himself that he was different, that he would not let anything go to his head…and then his parents would be proud of him, and he would be liked by people; they would thank him, like the vet service he provided. In a perfect world, all that would be true. To shift from ego to super-ego, wasn't really something that was within Paul; he had a great respect for life, (animal and human).

The people of the world made decisions everyday that were impactful, important, and Paul was certain that the "worldly decisions" would involve money, power, nations; and millions of lives were at stake. But the decisions that awaited Paul would be no less important to the individual involved. He was pretty certain, anyone influenced by The Healing – would find it much more important than a national, or worldly decision!

That was why Paul had to be particularly careful, he could not squander this gift; as far as he was concerned he was the "President of Nothing – but the Shaman of Men". There were all kinds of angles and things to consider:

Impacting the present – or the future; this could be catastrophic if not considered.

The laws of nature – Theory of Natural Selection could be considered.

Impacting the loved ones – it's enough to give someone else a heart attack!

Frightening the public – there was no way to explain; what couldn't be explained.

Money and power – What wealth wouldn't pay for a second chance.

Evangelism – The religious implications that could be exploited.

Multi-denominationalism – The various wars by religion were historic too.

Paul would have to take all of the above into consideration. It was a lot of work, responsibility, and the consequences of his decisions would last long after him. It reminded him of the saying, *"With great power – comes great responsibility"* from the movies he had seen. But the twist was – this wasn't a movie…this was real people that would find his gift both as a blessing and a sin. Would a man that has prepared, at peace with himself and his maker, that has lived a full life – appreciate you bringing him back? To live long enough to die from cancer or some other worldly disease; and suffer a second death – Paul wouldn't want that. He didn't think anyone else would appreciate that either.

What was to be his guide? What was to be his compass? How could he justify saving someone that later took someone else's life? How could he sleep at night, knowing he had created some, "FrankenPaul" or worse? He could simply "Freud" this to death and after forty or fifty years, maybe he could make some sense of how to be sure in the use of The Healing. He finally had to simply put his trust into whomever gave him this gift. He would try to take in the situation, be responsible, and try his best to be worthy of such a gift.

Chapter 3

The phone awoke Paul in a jolt, (he hated that feeling that you're late, when you awaken). It almost was like some extra-sensory-perception that the day could hold some things that could be better off handled, if he only stayed in bed. His stomach rolled and gurgled; reminding him that he didn't eat much before going to bed the evening before. His head was deciding between a pastry, fruit, or a granola bar for breakfast; instead, the phone barked an urgent need for him to go in early – on a Saturday of all things.

"Paul, we really need to get out to Hauser to the Fire House, apparently the Fire Chief's got a licensed dog that is a registered care companion for his PTSD, somebody hit the dog with their car!" Paul's boss, and the owner of the clinic advised. Paul had his emergency kit bag, he got some clothes changed, hair brushed, and he was brushing his teeth as he exited his house. He kept a syringe of the diluted Pentobarbital, which was used to euthanize the animal if necessary. As he spat some toothpaste from his mouth, while driving, a teenager saw the white mucous and believed he was foaming at the mouth. Paul laughed to himself as he yelled back to the person in the rear-view mirror, "Ruff, Ruff!" he barked!

When Paul arrived, there was a crowd of about a dozen, some were just gawking on-lookers, some wanted to comfort the man, some wanted to comfort the dog. It was a dark German Shepherd with some dark black along it's back. As soon as Paul seen the animal, he knew he was too late, it had shuffled about probably for minutes, after the internal damage from the Jeep that had hit it earlier.

"Please, everyone, get back," Paul began to direct the crowd to allow his access. A couple firemen still in yellow Nomex began to assist pushing the crowd back to allow the vet to assess the situation.

The Fire Chief was shaking all over as he approached Paul, "Can you help Rex out?" he began. "The dog is everything to me, he stopped me from crossing at the fruit-stand; just in time for me, but the car hit him!" the Chief continued. The Chief pleaded, "If it's a matter of money, I can get some savings, and folks may help me out too," he promised Paul.

"No Chief," Paul began, "there is major intestinal damage, his vitals are going to be low, and I got here as soon as I could, but it may be too late, there may be nothing that I can do."

The man fell to the ground in a pile of anxiety, his heart finding the whole thing too much to handle. One of the Firefighters called 911, (although the delay would probably be fifteen minutes that Paul just drove). The young man began CPR, with Paul still hovering over the dog. After checking; Paul found the dog to be non-responsive, and his body was shutting down. He did the right thing and injected the dog into the vein, and about five seconds later the dog had expired quietly without pain.

Paul advised his onlooking crowd that there was extensive damage, and the animal could not be saved. He asked a couple of the men to please load the animal into the back of his pick-up truck. There was a tarp in the back and Paul used it to fold it over and cover the dog laying on the other side of the tarp. Looking back from the pick-up, Paul could see the valiant efforts of the Firefighters to save their Chief.

With both of the firemen changing out positions of chest compressions and giving breaths to the Chief, after a very long five minutes, the men were exhausted. The AED arrived, and they hooked the Chief up to it, after peeling the paper off and sticking the leads to the Chief's chest. There was no heartbeat, so the machine verbally warned people to stand back, and a shock was administered…but to no avail. The man driving the Jeep that had hit the dog, began vomiting, people were crying, and the Chief was dead. They would all simply wait for the ambulance to arrive that was yelling a long way in the background.

Paul approached the body of the Chief that had previously been talking to him, he crouched down and said aloud, "Sorry Chief, I wish I could have saved your Rex!"

A woman nearby bellowed into tears as she heard Paul's statement, knowing how sorrowful Paul was for the tragedy. As Paul placed his palm upon the Chief's chest; in an effort to show care and compassion, a slight blue haze developed around his hand. Within a couple seconds, the Fire Chief regained consciousness and yelled, "REX!"

The dozen on-lookers yelled, "It's a miracle" as the Chief was helped to a sitting position. The Chief was crying, but he was breathing in between his sobs. The two Firemen were looking at each other with amazement, then looking at the Chief, then looking at Paul! Paul quickly shook the two firemen's hand and congratulated them on saving their Chief. The two, looked dumb-founded, but happy as they too broke into cheers and tears. Paul threw out a white-lie and advised he had to go. The crowd didn't put the thing together, but the CPR and AED didn't save the Chief's life. Paul knew it.

He hurried into his pick-up and cheered the firemen again as he drove off, and back to his house to get ready for work. Paul pulled away, but as he reached the McCullough Memorial Bridge to enter North Bend, his chest hurt sharply. Needing to pull over quickly, he turned to the Veteran Memorial layby, put it in park and took a second. He grabbed at what felt like serious indigestion or anxiety, but as the pain subsided, he focused on returning to driving into town. He arrived at his house, near Mingus Park. He went in and called the office advising them of the situation and status, and that he was going to shower, dress and see them in half an hour.

After a quick shower and some toast with huckleberry honey, Paul got dressed and went back out to the pick-up, locking the house as he exited. Upon arrival, he was disappointed that he couldn't help the service animal, he pulled the tarp back briefly. The dog was very well marked and had a bit of a diamond shape dark hair on his head. Paul was feeling sorrowful, so he stroked the dogs head, and said to himself, "Sorry boy, I couldn't help you this time".

The dog sprung to life! It howled more than a bark, the breed is more communicative than most but doesn't bark as much as people imagine; except to defend. "Rex, come here boy!" Paul hoped more than directed. The dog came to him, as Paul felt the chest pain reminder briefly. He dismissed it, and didn't think much of it, as he was so excited about the dog. He used his cell phone to call work and instead of driving to work, he put the dog into the cab of the pick-up and drove it back to Hauser.

As Paul pulled into the Fire House parking lot, he could see the ambulance, without any overhead lights flashing. That was a good sign, he thought as he turned off his vehicle; they will be taking him in for caution to check him out anyway. Paul could see the majority of the group had went into the Fire Station to celebrate the Chief's health and to console him on the loss of Rex.

Paul opened the door, to allow the dog to exit, but as he was now home and knew his surroundings, the dog ran quickly right into the Fire House! Paul heard the screams and excitement of the crowd before he got to the building entrance.

"You are truly a blessing," an older woman yelled, the Chief simply started crying again as he fell to his knees, kissing the dog that was now liking him in the face. "You saved Rex," the Chief blurted out, "I don't know how to thank you and if there is ever anything I can do, just let me know!"

Paul was confused, because if the internal injuries didn't kill Rex, the shot into his vein surely would have; this dog had no right to be alive, but he was happy to see the Chief and the crowd cheering his name. The dog and master were meant for each other, it was a miracle! By the time Paul made it back to the office, all the staff had heard the news that he had saved the service animal, and he received credit for summoning the ambulance or the AED, and it was just a whole lot of drama that he could have lived without.

Paul was concerned with what truly happened; he knew the truth and that dog should probably be no more alive than the Chief. Both were more than fortunate coincidences or timely first aid. It was crazy, the whole thing was timing; dealing with dogs, epidemic, stock markets and his 401k; Paul was really being tested here. He didn't get much sleep, dreaming of the cruise ship, and all the sickness that played out. The spin of the dream was the passengers turning into evil dead, coming after him; as nightmares go, it seemed great to awaken.

Reality was slapping him right in the face, this entire world seemed to be turning upside-down. Food markets were closing, gas was outrageous, and many weren't sure what their monetary status was; some elderly doctors, dentists, nurses, and health care had moved or not survived the Birdfire. All this chaos, and he was spending his thinking time on how a dog came back to life. Paul thought that the night sleep would do him good; secretly he hoped the whole previous day would have been a dream. He was pretty sure that the days that followed would not be as the previous; he dressed after showering and got ready for work as usual. He was now bicycling to work, gas seemed too expensive to waste when he only had about 18 blocks to bicycle. There were lots of hills and the Coos Bay area and most of the bicycle trip was simply coasting down hills, Paul figured the exercise would be good for him anyway.

When Paul got to work that day, the small crew of staff awaited his arrival. They had a local newspaper in hand with questions about the lead story on the front page. Apparently, the fire chief in Hauser had been called to a fire and rescued the family inside claiming heroic actions prior had saved him. Paul didn't make a big deal about the newspaper article, but to him it was a big deal. The office that day seemed to have a more positive and optimistic attitude towards its daily routine. It was a refreshing break from the catastrophic news and people's awareness about the world around them.

It wasn't long before the Sheriff's office contacted the veterinary clinic, advising that the dog the Chiefs had went bad, and bitten a child. Paul was just thankful that he didn't have to report to tranquilize the dog apparently a sheriff deputy had taken on the responsibility and shot the dog in the head, it was now dead, they are bringing the remains of the dog to the clinic to determine if there was any cause for it being rabid. Paul briefly stopped and considered why the Chiefs resurrection was positive and yet the dogs was negative. The news of the Chiefs heroism far outweighed the news of his dog and the death. Paul considered his interaction between the two in briefly dismissed it just as quickly. The whole thing appeared to be a Yang and Yang or positive and negative outcome. All seemed to have ended well; Paul dismissed the rest of the day as a good one.

The allegedly rabid dog arrived by the close of business that day, because Paul was the junior that fell upon him to conduct the tests and conclude the evidence; with regard to the dog's physical state. As the deputies brought the dog and placed it in the position the receptionist had requested, the rest of the crew for the day was leaving and Paul was left to perform the duty. It wasn't a difficult procedure, fluids from animal were taken and then placed in containers sealed, and then sent to a lab for analysis. Paul had performed the function many times before but because of his interaction with the dog previous days earlier he took the initiative to perform the autopsy. Paul half-way expected the dog to burst into life again, he was leery to say the least.

The internal organs of the animal seemed intact and nothing unusual too much; until Paul got to the animal's brain, there seem to be a small area affected that had turned green – the color was unusual and should not have been in the animal. It became obvious once the cranium was cracked. Since Paul couldn't account for it, he took some of the fluid for analysis and just described it as "unknown". He then took some photographic evidence and placed it in the animals file and then placed it on the desk for the secretary to file the following day. He wrapped the specimen's box and placed it on the secretary's desk as well for shipment to the lab. The green color puzzled him since he had never encountered anything like it as a veterinarian. Paul secretly wondered what Hauser Fire Chief's head would look like if you were to crack his cranium. Paul was pretty sure that his head wouldn't have any of the green fluid, but the chiefs head would certainly be bigger after the rescue of the family and all the media.

Paul closed-up the veterinarian shop, turned on the alarm, quickly exited the door locking up behind him. He laughed to himself a little bit about all the primary and secondary actions that had taken place since he had reported to Hauser to help the chief's dog. As he got on his bicycle after unlocking it and headed home, his only thoughts were of the hill that he now had to climb to get back home. With each step of the pedals that moved forward, he wondered about the timing that had occurred, that propelled everything else forward this past week. Paul was ready for some routine, veterinarians rarely deal with critical issues; unless it was the person bringing in their pet – Paul liked those critical issues…he could handle them.

This other stuff that seemed to pop-up and catch him off-guard, he could live without. Paul was more of a private person; he liked helping animals. Critters seemed to appreciate his gentle touch and mannerism in healing them, Paul at least felt that way. Animals were often a pretty good judge of character too; Paul had seen animal abuse, cruelty, and had remembered what his folks had said about people, and the care of pets. He also knew that sometimes the best thing to do for a pet was to euthanize it, humanely take the hurt away. Sure, it was a last resort, most of the time it was not an option. But when the ache in their eyes and sound of their noises, are crying for relief from inoperable pain; Paul was an executioner.

Regretfully, sometimes triage of animals, (especially numerous) requires a judgement of prioritizing treatment. It seemed like a political answer to, "Which animals do you put to sleep, and which do you simply kill?" When Paul was hunting deer or elk, he was killing them, not for sport – but for food. He couldn't understand "trophy hunters" that would limit their kill to only the biggest…they would starve! What seemed difficult was pets often are part of the family unit, and their determined death can require adjusting or mourning too.

If two people bring in two different pets, are they not equal for the need for care? It wasn't a simple process; a five-year old girl's turtle versus a five-year old girl's tarantula – which would need care first? Both of the toddlers would cry at the loss of the pet. It didn't make it any easier prioritizing care. Would Paul find it easier to put the spider down, than the turtle? Absolutely! He would show love, care, compassion, and empathy to the little girl and then the arachnophobia would enjoy putting the bug in a bag to stomp! It was all part of the job, he thought.

Paul remembered a real ass-hole had brought in his dog for routine and scheduled annual vaccination. Regretfully, he couldn't control the animal, he hadn't been trained properly, and it got loose from him, killing a six-month old kitten that an adorable little girl had brought in for an eyewash. It was a dreadful, and unnecessary event that could have been prevented if people took proper care of their pets.

Paul wondered what psychological trauma was imposed upon the little girl that day; it's tough to put a price on things like that. One thing seemed apparent…the innocent little girl that had love in her heart, and a kitten in her lap; was exposed to a bloody and traumatic experience that resulted in the death of her first pet. It didn't mean that he should not treat the dog. Sometimes Paul hated his job, (but like most people,) he loved his job; especially when it lights up the face of the child's pet he saved. He always thought it would be cool to have a magic wand, (like in the movies) and be able to wave it and cure or heal the pet (or person) completely!

Chapter 4

Paul deserved a damn day off! For crying-out-loud; it was a Sunday. The phone didn't seem to care about the hell of a week that he had prior. It would ring, leave a message, and then ring some more! He just gave up and answered it, there was nothing like speaking to law enforcement when you first wake up. You instantly try to think of anything you've done recently that could be criminal. In this case he was glad that he was not involved but hated that he was neck deep in post-involvement.

"Hey Paul," I'm sorry to wake you on a weekend, but you are the only one we could imagine contacting, under these circumstances," the Deputy advised after introducing himself over the phone. The owner and your partner at the clinic, was in a terrible vehicle accident and apparently broke his neck, he's at the hospital, but he didn't make it." We will have to contact his family, but you may be able to help break the news to them…and handle the business, I guess?"

"Oh, my God," Paul began, I'm so sorry to hear about this, is he the only victim?" "I can meet you at the hospital, I'll be right there, I'll drive."

"We figured you would drive sir," the deputy stated the obvious, "Thanks again, we'll see you when you get here, they will direct you to the ICU when you arrive."

Paul laughed to himself as he hung up the phone, "I'll drive" he said, mocking himself. He simply used the bicycle most of the time, with the price of gas near ten bucks a gallon. He felt sorry for all the folks that had gas guzzlers, but then he remembered riding in his brother Lance's Camaro, and it would be worth ten bucks!

Arriving at the hospital, a Coos County Deputy met him and escorted him to the Senior Deputy that he had apparently spoke to earlier. The three men went to the body of Mr. Spencer that was now covered with a sheet. Removing the sheet, Dick Spencer didn't look too bad, he was pale and light colored, but it wasn't a bloody mess. The truck had hit him squarely in a T-bone and the impact broke his neck instantly. Not a bad way to go, if you had to, Paul supposed.

"We're contacting his family next; do you know the name of his wife?" the Deputy asked. "Are there kids that may need cared for, were you close to the family?" the Deputy continued asking questions before allowing Paul to answer. He felt like he was being interrogated.

"Here is an idea," Paul began calmly, "how about you treat me like a victim too, since I'm certainly not a suspect." "His wife's name is Diane, they have two children, age eight and ten," Paul focused toward the Senior Deputy, "Yes, we were partners, he sold fifty percent to me last year to gain funding for the expansion, and he had life insurance that his wife would sure need help handling."

The Senior Deputy caught on and apologized for the energetic and young Deputy that had been firing questions. He politely excused the other Deputy, asking him to please contact the family…with more caring this time, bring the wife, and help with the kids being taken care of somewhere. He advised they would place the body in the morgue, and if Paul would accompany him to meet Diane there, it would be greatly appreciated. Paul liked this new and improved approach by a veteran deputy. He shook his head and agreed, they took documents from the hospital and wheeled the body to the staging area on the basement floor. The Deputy advised he would be preparing for Diane's arrival, asking if Paul had any last words he would like privately with the deceased. After nodding and agreeing, Paul approached the body, and the Deputy departed.

Paul felt so sorry for the family, Diane and the kids would probably sell the business and move away, it would impact the community too. Paul uncovered the face of his partner, folding the sheet back slowly, folding it with care, he began to weep. Chewing the ass of the dead man, Paul said, "What the hell Dick, you're leaving us all with a hell of a mess fella." Paul's hand on his own forehead, he knelt over the body, weeping on his hand, which was on Dick's dead forehead.

There was some type of blue heat that seemed to resonate, and an instant later, Dick sat up, staring at Paul – who couldn't help but stare back! Dick was ALIVE! The two stared at each other with their mouths open – that was when Dick's neck straightened; and Paul fell back on his ass!

"What the hell, where am I, and what are you doing here Paul…hey where are my clothes damn it!" Dead Dick was speaking!

"Hey, what the hell Dick," Paul answered the undead man, "you were dead, the Deputy called Diane, he needed me here…dude, you were dead!" Paul picked himself up but kept some distance from Dick now.

"Oh my God…Diane is coming to see you Dick, and she's expecting you to STILL be dead," Paul thought to himself out loud. "What the hell are we gonna do?" "You gotta get out of here Dick, and I gotta tell that Deputy out there that all is well; while you make a getaway!"

Undead Dick smiled and said, "No, I have to let her know everything is okay, and so am I, she'll understand, I'll just break it easy to her."

Paul laughed cynically, "You idiot, a doctor, nurses, and law enforcement have all documented your death, you had a broken neck…you can't break anything to her, you're going to break her heart and she'll need a hospital!" Paul continued, "You need to get to my place, they won't look for you there, I'll say a hospital staff came and took the body, now GO!"

Dick found some white hospital gowns in a drawer and began to dress, while Paul spit on his finger and wiped it down his eye like tears, and exited the room, walking over to a desk where the Deputy was sitting. Paul waited to make eye contact, then wiped his eye and looked downward sadly. He then went over and sat at a padded chair, picking up a magazine nervously, he waited for the fireworks to begin.

It was only about ten minutes and the tearful and mournful wife of Paul's partner appeared, the kids must have been with a sitter. Paul wasn't much of an actor, so he tried the spittle trick again, hoping he could still act as though Dick were dead. Diane saw him immediately and ran to him in an embrace that Paul returned. "I'm so very sorry Diane, I will be available to help you in any way," Paul said as he finally broke the hug that seemed long enough. Diane reached up and wiped the spittle away from Paul's eye, not knowing what the heck it really was, but it was sincere.

"You seem more like family than a partner, Paul" Diane sobbed. "I just don't know what to do, we didn't plan on this, who does?" Diane asked the rhetorical question. "I'll have to contact all his family, and the bills, the taxes, oh God," she collapsed, but was caught by Paul.

The Deputy helped by getting her some water, the two of them guided her to be seated at the nearby sofa lounge across the hall. The Deputy did a great job relieving her of some details and letting her know that the Sheriff's Office would be ensuring the investigation would be available soon. He also relieved her, letting her know that the intersection evidence appeared to suggest the right of way was her husbands…there would be a possible lawsuit against the carrier. The whole nightmare seemed like something that Paul would never want to go through himself. Lastly, the Deputy advised they would need an autopsy as a matter of routine, and he wanted to know if Dick was under any medication.

Paul interrupted the inquisition with a bit of an interjection, "Do you think Diane could see Dick now?" he said firmly, more than asking a question.

"Certainly," the Deputy caught on, "we'll just take you to him now Ma'am" the Deputy blurted. "We are certainly so very sorry to put you through this Diane," he continued.

"It's Mrs. Spencer," she corrected him and seem to turn the tide of the conversation. She got up firmly, but Paul still had her hand to help balance her. "Thank you, take me to him now, I'll need some privacy or course," Mrs. Spencer was now giving directions.

The Deputy walked toward the door, motioning for them to follow. He opened the door and Paul reached around Diane to help hold her for what was about to happen, (although Paul wasn't certain what was going to happen himself). As the Deputy opened the door, stepping through he approached a drawn curtain with a gurney clearly on the other side. The Deputy jerked the curtain with authority, approached the gurney and grabbed the sheet delicately, as he pulled it back to reveal six pillows.

"I'll give you a minute," the Deputy said quietly and remorseful as he blindly turned away, not noticing the pillows. He turned to walk away, when Mrs. Spencer grabbed his arm and spun him back around to reveal the pillows.

"Well…I'm waiting" was all Mrs. Spencer had to say.

"Where's the body?" the poor Deputy began, always state the obvious he thought, "it was here before, you saw it" the Deputy said as he looked blankly at Paul.

"Don't look at me," Paul began, "I don't work here, I didn't bring it in, I did see Dick here with the Deputy."

"And were they talking," the poor widow sneered, "Can someone PLEASE find Dick!" She exhausted, "I'm not having a good day today, can someone help me find him?"

"That won't be necessary Ma'am," the Deputy assessed, "they were going to move the body to the Morgue, so that's where he's at I'm afraid." The Deputy offered to take them to the Morgue. He got on his radio mic and asked where the deceased was relocated. There was a lot of silence that followed. A response was slow to be heard, but the new deputy that Paul had met earlier finally answered up.

"Sir, the deceased is located at the basement level, on a gurney, behind a curtain, near the lounge furniture; after being moved from ICU". It was sad to hear, Paul was having a hard time not laughing hysterically. The Senior Deputy responded with a "that's a negative at that location".

"Sir, have you checked, because that's where I left him," the newer Deputy said in earnest.

"I'm there now, and we have a missing corpse then," the confused Senior Deputy advised. He calmly keyed the mic and said, "get the hospital to lock down, start at the top searching and I'll work my way up from the basement."

They were searching for Dick high and low and he was just arriving at Paul's address. Paul had shown him the turtle that held the door key, and Dick Spencer rolled in, headed for the refrigerator.

Paul wasn't sure if hiding Dick was such a great idea, it even sounded bad. He wasn't sure about anything, about the time the heartburn returned, it took him by surprise in its intensity. He held his chest tightly, as if to hold back the pain, but many a man has found the response as natural as useless. The pain left as quickly as it came, leaving Paul to wonder if he had something wrong, or if it was an anxiety attack. Maybe, it was the first (delayed) Birdfire attacking his body; perhaps he hadn't escaped it as he previously imagined.

Diane finally gave up, she advised the Deputies, to please call her when they find her husband's body. She had no idea what to tell the kids, she didn't make a practice of lying to them, but she didn't know when she could truthfully tell them that their father had died in an automobile accident. They would be devastated, so Diane decided to take the time to call the schools to advise she would be taking the kids out of school for a week or more. The Principal seemed very caring and understanding, offering any assistance and homework that would be requested.

While Diane waited for the law enforcement to decide if they had "abuse to a corpse" or "kidnapping" or something else entirely; Paul headed home to meet up with Dick. He was enjoying a pastrami on some artesian bread that he had warmed in the microwave, it smelled delicious. Paul hadn't eaten, but he remembered the fact about the time the aroma of the bread hit him when he came in the house. He wasn't sure that the undead would consume a sandwich, he hadn't seen all the TV shows about the living dead for nothing. He thought he should get the forty-caliber pistol ready if needed, from the closet, and then he would speak to Dick.

"Okay," Paul said as he tucked the pistol into the small of his back, "what the hell do you remember Dick?"

"I was driving," Dick began, "then I woke up in the hospital, with you beside me".

"That's it…you woke up?" Paul shook his head in disbelief. "There has to be something in between, there is a lot of time you're missing here, Dick?"

Dick sighed, took another bite and mumbled a compliment on the contents of the fridge and his home-made sandwich. "I got nothing," Dick said with his mouth still chewing".

"Well, what are we gonna do here, you need to go home, you can't stay here with me forever, their looking for your body out there damn it!" Paul blasted.

"I know," Dick proclaimed, "I'll simply have you invite my wife over here and we'll explain everything to her!"

"Oh no!" Paul exclaimed, "you're not drawing me into this, I'm a conflict of interest here, they will all think I'm trying to do something illegal with the business. You need to come up with another, better plan, that doesn't involve me."

"Okay," Dick tried plan "B" on Paul, 'take me to our cabin out by Reedsport, I'll stay there until you get Diane and bring her out to meet me."

"Well, it's not perfect, but it's better, just keep me out, as much as possible please," Paul pleaded. "We don't want to alarm everybody, and make a big deal about this," he concluded.

"I don't know how I'm alive Paul," a sad face took over Dick. He buried his head in his hands and began to cry. "I was going to see a woman that I've been having an affair with Paul," Dick admitted. "I'm unworthy to be alive, I should be dead, maybe I should just take my own life and then you could say you found it here?" Dick floated the unbearable thought.

"Don't be stupid," Paul quickly yelled loudly, "suicide is the permanent solution to a temporary problem, and it would kill Diane and the kids! "No," Paul advised, "you're gonna be the best damn Dad of the Year, and husband too, you're gonna break that crap off immediately".

"You're right Paul, I've been given a second chance that most people never get," Dick decided. "You are a true friend, thank you for being a wonderful man too!" Dick said as he dried his eyes. "Let's get out to the cabin, I'm ready to put a fork in me and call it done."

"Okay," Paul agreed, "but you can't ever use that metaphor again Dick!" "Maybe you can cook up something in that rejuvenated brain on the way to tell everyone, cause I'm fresh out of ideas," Paul said as they headed out the door. Paul suggested that Dick take his vital signs, to make sure he was okay, (Paul clutching the forty in his back). Everything checked out, all the vitals seemed good, at least Paul wasn't going to have to kill undead Dick. This was a crazy adventure that Paul thought, no one could make this crazy adventure up. About half way to Reedsport, Paul began to do the math; he wondered if the pain he felt was coincidental, or just timing after he laid hands on someone, (or their dog). Did he bring Dick back to life, there were more questions than answers? He would find it difficult to drive, hold his pain in, and think about what the heck was going on. The trip to

Reedsport is not a long one, but it would now seem to be a hurdle for Paul. He would later remember it as one of the longest drives in his life, Paul was doing his best to just get through this!

Chapter 5

The two fugitives jumped into the pick-up and headed into the Coos Counties most wanted list and bound for Reedsport to hide away in a cabin along the Umpqua River, if Paul could make it. They were careful to drive very legally, allowing little to chance. Paul had known and respected Dick as a friend and partner; he had every reason to help him, (he felt somewhat responsible for him and the whole predicament). Paul had grown up around John Day, Oregon; and he would periodically watch oncoming drivers, throwing up a wave from his steering wheel in return. Sometimes, he simply waved to be friendly, because everyone around Seneca waved and no one did it much in Coos Bay anymore.

Dick saw an oncoming vehicle that had the official state government plate, yellow in background color; as the vehicle approached their pick-up, Paul waved at the driver – unknowing if the driver would return the wave.

"What the hell are you doing," Dick spouted, "are you trying to draw attention to us?" He went on about how they need to be under the radar, when Paul truthfully had more to worry about than Dick.

"Just chill-out Dick," Paul semi-ordered, "we're going to be there soon". "You need to be thinking about what story we're going to come up with to justify you being alive, escaped from the morgue, obstructed justice by fleeing and hiding; oh, and then there is always what to tell your wife and kids." The shock-wave of truthful terror could be read in his face, reality had taken a crap on him and life suddenly seemed a little more difficult than it had ever been in his entire life. Paul readvised that he was simply driving to assist Dick; but secretly he had to help him out of the jam he had put him in.

"Okay, how does this sound," Dick prepared to introduce a plan, "I had an allergic reaction to something, it stopped my heart, I died, CPR and AED were utilized, but you pounded on my chest in futile dismay, and it must have awoken me?" "I must have been unconscious and got a ride to the cabin from a tourist," Dick smiled…it made him look sinister.

"Whatever, Dick," Paul smirked, "it's your story, I'm just going to help facilitate it." "How am I supposed to get Diane to the cabin, and how do I even know where the damn thing is?"

"I finally come to my senses and called you on your cell," Dick smiled sinisterly again, "it sounds perfect!" Paul was going to pull the vehicle over to tell him to "never smile!" Dick thanked Paul again, so he nodded affirmatively.

Following Dick's directions, they had arrived at an old cabin that he had purchased through a friend for a song. It was somewhat in need of some TLC, but the Spencer's had found restoring it was a family outing for a weekend now and then. Dick unlocked the door and walked in, Paul followed cautiously, (still confirming the location of the forty, and tucking the handgun in more firmly).

Dick came directly face to face with Diane, she apparently had parked in the back and needed to get away from the house and kids; she had obviously been crying and eating some grapes. The only thing Paul saw was Diane's look of horror as she swallowed a grape, it added more fright to her face! She tried gulping, but the grape lodged in her windpipe. She hit the floor like a sack of potatoes! Paul wasn't sure if she had fainted at the sight of Dick, fainted due to lack of oxygen, or if Dick was smiling again!

Paul thought to himself, there are clowns to the left, jokers to the right, and here he was stuck in the middle – like the lyrics to some song by "_Stealers Wheel_" he yelled out, "Dick she's choking!" Dick grabbed Diane and began the Heimlich-Maneuver, it resulted in the grape shooting out and hitting Paul in the face, and then falling to the floor! In a second, Diane gasped for life, and she began breathing, but hadn't regained consciousness.

Dick and Paul got her to the sofa and Paul fetched a glass of water, while Dick was caressing her face, talking quietly to her. Diane awoke to the nightmare she had thought was only just a dream; she screamed into Dick's face and then embraced him in a tight bear-hug that seemed to take his breath. Before she could get the question out, Dick began to spew the lie he had prepared to explain the situation, modifying it to suit his needs. Paul said he picked him up in the pick-up and took him to the cabin he had almost already arrived at.

After Dick's crappy story, Diane got on the phone to a babysitter to have the kids brought out to the cabin's address via Taxi. They were unaware of the death of Dick, and the near death of Diane; and so, the charade continued. The adults decided to not tell the kids, and to ask the hospital why they misdiagnosed a broken neck. The trio would stick to their stories, and no one would be any wiser. Paul liked the idea, but he knew the whole thing was a façade.

Paul had cancelled work for the crew at the vet clinic. He apologized to the Spencer's, but it wasn't necessary, and they confirmed their appreciation and now even more personal love for their family and having their Dick back. Paul headed home after a barrage of questioning by deputies. On the way home he wondered, "What would have happened if Dick hadn't been quick to CPR, or if it would have failed…what would that have resulted in?"

The theory of Dick dead, not dead, and then Diane dead, but not dead; was jamming up his mind. This whole entire thing made his head hurt, but his heart hurt too. Paul was glad to finally get back to the house and put away the sandwich material that Dick had left out. He wondered if he was most hungry, exhausted, full of anxiety, or if he could even sleep? He felt like he just needed a break from life, for about a week on a desert island. He could definitely use the down-time, maybe even meet a girl, like in all the songs.

He settled for two sodas, and a couple pieces of leftover fried chicken, followed by a couple "PM pain-relievers" and some soft music to attempt a nap. He was hoping the chicken would drift him off to slumber, and the sleep aide would kick in; creating his mock-island feeling in his head, REM sleep. It worked for a few hours too, until he felt a dream. He hadn't experienced a dream like it before. It began slowly and crept into his subconscious, then it was like experiencing pain in his chest, he grabbed at it, although his hand would pass through his body! It was enough to awaken him, and he experienced that feeling of verification if you're in a dream still, or not. His chest didn't hurt anymore, but he wondered about the ghostly hand that he had used to clutch himself…it was damn disturbing. Too disturbing to sleep, he decided, and got up to take a nice hot shower and climb back into bed, attempting one more of the pills, he found it easier to swallow than the past few days.

The next few hours seemed relentless attempts to get some sleep. Why is it that we are supposed to sleep, we need to sleep, but sometimes it's so futile because of whatever happened during the *non-sleep* part of our life? Granted, Paul had more than the average crud happening to him; and lately he just longed for the average. People like routines, they know what time to be at work, be at the school, be on time for appointments, and when change smacks them or jams-up their mind, like Paul lately; it's uncomfortable. Paul needed a down week, so he thought he would go in to work and let them know he needed to take a week off. That subtle thought was just the ticket to slide Paul into a sleep-slumber that he needed.

To hope for no dreams was fool-hearty; but Paul did seem to limit them to minimal proportions. When he finally did awaken; Paul had about two seconds of, "maybe it was all just a bad dream" before reality crushed his hopeful wish. The darn cell phone started vibrating and dancing around on the nightstand. Paul wasn't sure which was worse, the rattle, scuffle, vibrating, or silent mode – or just plain ring? He grabbed the phone – already angry at it.

"Yes, this is Paul," he baited the unknown number, waiting for a response.

"Hi, this is Dr. Simmons," the voice was trying hard to sound soothing, a little too hard; "I was the performing physician at the call of death for Mr. Spencer, and I just had some questions I'd really like to run by you, if we could meet?"

Paul was about fed up, he really didn't have time to play doctor, and he was honestly stressed out from all this, but he did pick up the phone angry, "I have just one question for you doctor, did you perform an autopsy on Mr. Spencer?"

"Well," the doctor started to feel more defensive, "I didn't have time to perform an autopsy of the body."

"Well," Paul laughed cynically, "maybe it was a damn good thing that you didn't!" Paul pounded the nail on the coffin, "You will find the Sheriff maybe forwarding documents to our business attorney that may indicate malpractice, so I can't discuss this now."

A very worried and quiet voice came back, being the kind of soothing tone and heartfelt apology that Paul enjoyed hearing the vast improvement. There would be no more of this, Paul was determined to put his foot down, (or up someone's keester). As soon as he put the cell phone down, the damn thing began jumping about again. It was one of the girls in the office, Cara was advising that a dog was near death and that Mr. Spencer couldn't be reached. Paul confirmed he would come down to assist in about fifteen minutes and threw the cell phone gently onto the pillow on the bed, in an angry and defiant manner.

    The dog emergency turned out to be the neighbor kid finally admitting that he gave his neighbor's dog a bar of chocolate. The sweet treat had completely messed up the guts of a poor little Scottie. Paul fixed Elvis, with a simple double shot – one elixir down the gullet and one injected into his ass. About two minutes later, while the owner was caressing Elvis; he shot crap two and a half feet across the room and into the blouse of the owner! It was that real slick stuff too, it coated her neckline and then continued to shoot a straight shot on the wall behind her!

    Paul looked astonished, (although he knew the desired effect had been achieved) and simply replied, "sometimes that happens!" After charging the emergency visit, the office girl came up to Paul with rags and volunteered to clean up after the x-lax factor. Paul thanked the new girl Cara, and then proceeded to draw up a quick thank you note to her that opened the office for an emergency call. He tucked a couple twenty dollars in the note, to show his appreciation. Then he took the two bills out and replaced it with a fifty; after remembering the Jetstream clean-up. He let the girl know that Dr. Spencer would be out of the office and he anticipated himself being only on call for emergencies. They often would then make referrals to another vet when unavailable. She thanked him for letting her know, and Paul handed her the envelope that simply said, "Thanks!"

    Paul headed back to the house on his bike, (knowing the formidable hill to climb to his house awaited him). As he peddled slowly and harder up the hill; Paul thought that it was a good thing that Dick was alive and handy to have gotten the grape out of Diane. He supposed that he probably would have gotten it out if Dick hadn't been there. But if Dick hadn't died, Diane wouldn't have gasped, Paul almost tipped the darn bike over dwelling on "what if's?"

    Finally arriving at the house, he stowed the bike in the garage and made his way into the house. Someone once had told Paul of the hundreds of thousands of gallons that Coos Bay roofs dispel, and drainage is key…due to the many hills surrounding the area. It was like the rest of Oregon was having some snow and ice, driving conditions were bad, but in Coos Bay it would just simply be raining again, (day after day usually in winter). Paul liked not having to scrape the frost off his window, not having to "chain-up" and being able to ride a bike…even in winter.

The past few days were wearing on Paul, he was hoping no emergencies would hit for a couple days at least. He laughed at himself a little as he got to the kitchen and poured a glass of milk. He wasn't so much of a proud man, he didn't crave power or wealth. He reflected quickly the last few days and the crazy things that had occurred and he laughed at himself again. It was a bit of a roller-coaster ride, with some pitfalls that only yielded questions and no answers. There were several wonderful Chinese restaurants in North Bend and Coos Bay, so he called his favorite and ordered, knowing it would take him three days to eat all the food they would send. He knew he had a beer still in the fridge, (if Dick didn't drink it.)

Stupidly, he had ordered without checking his wallet to make sure he had enough cash, (obtaining cash seemed to be a bit trickier since the Birdfire) and he confirmed the amount to cover the order, but his fifty-dollar bill had been given to the assistant. Within twenty minutes the knock on the door assured a cozy evening watching a video, and a Chinese banquet. Paul liked to cook, and he most often cooked to save money. But now and then, if he had to order take-out, Chinese was king!

After watching a video, munching on the variety before him; Paul took the last tug on the bottle of beer, and the last bit always tasted just a little bitter, probably because it was no longer cool and refreshing. Paul thought he would top off the taste buds with a fortune cookie, he popped open the packaging, broke the cookie in half and tugged at the fortune. Two fortunes had been crammed into the cookie, Paul thought it would be fun to think of a simple game. He thought, "My real fortune will be the second one I read".

The first fortune simply stated, "YOU ARE BLESSED". Paul laughed and grabbed the second paper, turning it over it again stated, "YOU ARE BLESSED".

Raised religiously, Paul believed blessings are from God, they are not to be questioned, and you thank him via prayer each evening. Paul stopped his drifting mind and stopped to ask himself if he had asked a blessing before this feast. He knew that the answer isn't something you can lie about…he stopped, knelt, and closed his eyes, beginning to pray:

"Thank you oh Lord for this food that I should have asked you to bless before consuming, thank you for the past, present, and the future, for whatever it brings, I know you are with me. Thank you for the many blessings you have bestowed upon me, a humble sinner." Amen.

Paul felt entirely better, he believed his soul; perhaps was as hungry, as his body was for that fried rice. Taking one of those blue over the counter sleep aids, he drifted into a soft slumber. When in college, Paul remembered the Psych course that talked about dreams. Often dreams start with a simple wish, the interpretation that followed seemed to have either sex or your mother/father implicated. Paul thought a lot of people probably dreamt of winning a lottery and millions of dollars. Paul always hoped none of them would pray for money, because the love of money was known as the root of all evil, why would you pray for something that was earthly, and evil?

It seemed simple to Paul, that the average Joe, probably couldn't fathom a hundred million dollars. He was also certain, that if there was an amount that someone could win, like a hundred million dollars it would turn the best of men into the worst. In any case, Paul believed prayer should be revered, nothing that is evil should ever be prayed for; he felt it strongly. He believed in carrying a life commitment to prayer, to remember those in need, to ask for the healing hand of God upon the ill or dying. As he loved and cherished his talking to God each evening, he also may take a few seconds throughout the day. The sunburst through the rain, the rainbow, the lunch that someone shared with him, the list was endless and random.

Paul wasn't sure about all the different religions, frankly, he didn't care. If they were peaceful in their prayer, and it could perhaps be directed to God via their prophet, that was great. Paul didn't judge them, it wasn't for him to do so. He didn't care about the different varieties of Christianity, everyone had their favorite church. It was more about the prayer – than the people. Paul thought, "If a person doesn't pray their entire life, but they are kind, helpful to others, and believed – would they be judged for not praying?" Paul practiced a little differently, he simply went on faith and believed that God was Love. It was enough for him, and he liked having his talks with God as he walked through the life that he was granted from above.

Paul laughed out loud, he thought it would be great to have one of those tents that travel the South on the power of prayer, and when it came time to take the offering…the preacher should tell the folks in the audience to, "Take a dollar out of the basket and keep it!" If the tent held a couple hundred people; it would cost them that much money. After about five of these shows you would have invested a thousand dollars; but if you truly impacted that many people, a thousand followers could be a strong base to spread the gospel. Paul laughed out loud again at the thought of it. He thought this was a bit too deep for a vet, (it was his way of often dismissing things that weren't within his control).

Some institutions, and all religions; judge people by their choice of religion. When Paul was growing up, when he traveled; he went to different buildings of belief. There were Synagogues, Temples, Churches, and all kinds of names applied to the buildings. Paul would secretly attend service, (dressed as appropriately as he could). Someone of Jewish faith presented him with a neat little hat when he attended a service, but the Hebrew from the Tora was a challenge for him to understand. A very devout service however, and there was some Latin in a Cathedral once that he didn't understand; but it too, was a devout service.

He always donated to whichever building that he attended. He didn't really find any service that turned down money. He thought it strange since he wasn't really "giving unto Caesar, that which is of Caesar". Some services in the evening turned out to be AA or NA meetings, but Paul still attended. He wasn't forced to speak, so he simply thanked everyone for their sharing.

It's easy to see religions judging other religions; simply put, they are the only "true" path; they will remind you of it often. Paul didn't mind, he had seen, listened, and even read many of the different religious texts; there was always some peaceful meaning when read. But caution was always used, (and a little common sense by Paul.) It would not do, (for example) to be reading the Tora aloud on a bus in Utah, nor would he attend a service at a Mosque with a bible in hand. Paul found most religions enjoyed seeing him nod positively, (in an up and down motion.) He simply would smile, bow his head slightly, nod, and look up for a response. Most seemed to enjoy the non-conversational gesture. One of the Taoists didn't raise his head from the bow, so Paul kept his head down too…it went on for about five minutes.

Paul tried to respect people, (even those he didn't understand.) He knew better than to disrespect their religion, people will fight and kill in the name of their religion. Paul had the opportunity to attend a Wiccan service, (outdoors of course) which included a lot of earth-based things that resembled the Native American service he had previously attended. Perhaps religions were a lot closer than they would ever want to admit. Paul had come to some conclusion that religion itself, was a positive glue that helped keep society in communication and from tearing each other apart. He believed there were both good and bad histories of any religion. It was probably appropriate that Paul would have this outlook on life and the religion that surrounds it.

Chapter 6

Paul took a good part of a week off from work, but he almost dread returning to it and wondering what was said, who believed what, and was normality lost completely forever. If there is one thing that can make a person comfortable, it's without a doubt, routine. That nice and cozy feeling that you know what is going to happen today, and you're prepared for it. No drama, no politics, no religion, no accidents…just the expected routine. People work at a career, (although sometimes in more than one job) and after getting up, going to work for thirty years, they feel good enough to retire. Regretfully, some fall into decay in health, or they start watching the boob-tube and never seem to realize sloth, has taken them a couple years later.

Paul cruised downward on his bike, enjoying the "flying" feeling as he sat back and let gravity shuttle his butt to work. He was like so many coastal Oregonians, he loved cruising on his bicycle. Some kids never grow up, Paul continued to enjoy his bike. Other adults would never grow up; but want the thrill of speed…and the Hog passed him like a ghost. Paul grabbed hold to prepare for the wind, but it had already hit and run. He controlled the bike well, and it was necessary for experience to take the wheel for a brief second.

Cruising into work, he did the usual dismount; while still standing on one side of the bike and on one pedal, he coasted into the bike rack and locked it in with a smooth motion. He came in the door, smiling at least, next was some surprise party the team had planned. As they scared him with a hearty cheer, he was a bit gun-shy; hiding behind the door for a split second. He then recoiled, and he saw the cake and balloons, and Dick with Diane; both smiling. It was a joyous thing to behold, and Paul could feel the normality returning. Today was going to be a good day, he thought to himself.

Since they had been off, they needed to catch up on some pet maintenance that could be backlogged. That meant neutering a bunch of young animals, and then volunteering at pet shelters to cut some more neutering. It was all a bunch of routine, but the surgeries weren't considered a priority or vital. It still was a nasty job that the Dr. receives no real gratification or thanks from anyone, (or any pet!)

Paul went to the County seat of Coquille, where the courthouse is that all the public must report for jury duty. He showed the lady at the desk his credentials and identification, she thanked Paul for helping at a new pet shelter. She gave him the address, and advised that she would call ahead, Mrs. Johnson would expect him. He drove right to the house, or what would resemble a house, until you opened the door. Once he knocked, Paul simply tried to enter the domicile. As soon as he got inside, a vicious yell from what could only have been Mrs. Johnson could be heard throughout the house, "Don't let the kittens out, close the damn door, what are you born in a barn!"

Paul apologized aloud to the voice, although he hadn't met Bulla yet, closing the door he introduced himself to about sixty cats and kittens, "Hi, I'm the vet, Paul Baldwin, here to look in on you and the kitties!"

"You have experience with pussies," Bulla asked, as she turned the corner?

"Well, yes Ma'am," Paul now reached out his hand to shake hers, "I've been a partner of the Vet Clinic in Coos Bay for a few years."

"Did you go to Eugene or Corvallis for schooling," Bulla interrogated him, "well, are you a duck or a beaver?"

Paul had lived here long enough to see the set-up and booby-trap coming. People in the area were devout supporters of either the green and gold; or the orange and black; she obviously had a preference. To befriend her, Paul took a different route, "Mrs. Johnson, I started at Blue Mountain in Pendleton, and we were the timber wolves, we eat beaver and duck for breakfast!'

The candid and stern nature seemed to turn the conversation, Bulla smiled, "that a boy, you saw the rivalry trap and didn't fall for it!" She advised she couldn't care less, and that any assistance from a vet would be greatly appreciated. She turned out to be the warmest, and most loving woman, Paul had ever come across. He wished she was thirty years younger, he liked her.

She escorted him around, introducing him to various named cats, and Paul was amazed how much she knew and remembered. Next, she took him to the upstairs, where the more ill, or hurt animals were; and Paul broke out his kit and served all that she pointed out. There was a bit of a cat urine and stench that Paul had to hold his breath a bit, and Bulla could tell he was near vomiting once. She took out a small vial container of lady's perfume, dabbed her finger and then stuck it right onto his mustache under his nose; it worked.

They finished the tour, treatment, and scheduling names for possible neutering and adoption soon, Bulla thanked Paul and was walking with him back to his rig to put his kit away and say farewell. It was almost six in the evening, Paul had been inside longer than he planned. As Bulla turned around the corner of the old house, a yellowjacket or some type of bee hit her in the neck and stung her. She swatted, but missed it, she mumbled something about being stung and Paul looked back at her and she was holding her neck. As Paul put his kit inside the rig, he turned and saw her collapse! He quickly went around to the jockey-box, (people in New York call them glove compartments) and grabbed the EpiPen and swung around the rig and headed for Mrs. Johnson. When Paul got to her, she was non-responsive. He quickly jabbed the pen into her thigh, through her pants and injected the life-saving liquid.

He then put his cell phone down and dialed for an emergency, leaving the line open. He was speaking to the 911dispatch, he let them know he had initiated the first aid. The Paramedics arrived and initiated CPR. It took the paramedics only a few minutes to get there, but it was too long. They tried to get her back with an AED, but she was walking in sunshine nowhere on earth.

The phone call when Paul got home confirmed his worst suspicions, Mrs. Johnson had expired, there would be a funeral next week. Paul was asked to attend, to meet the family, but he declined. His nights were filled with fluffy-damn nightmares of him grabbing Bulla's hand at the funeral and her sitting up for all her relatives and family to see what Paul could do! It was crazy, and he wouldn't have any part of it. But he did write to the family and vowed to continue Bulla's work, at no cost, once a week; in memory of her love for animals. Flowers accompanied the arrangement, and Paul did receive a thank you card from the family.

It continued to remind Paul that there was life and death, both were part of God's plan; he worried that he should not tempt fate, or God. This seemingly apparent gift that had been the biggest blessing in two centuries for mankind – had to pick Paul. It was probably all for nothing, "Maybe, it's just my imagination," thought Paul. He began to become obsessed with reading of the bible elements that included bringing the dead back to life. He knew that today's science would not have it. But throughout the Bible it speaks of Jesus resurrection, it also included some others.

In the Bible, (1 Kings 17:17-24) Paul found the widow of Zarephath's son was raised by Elisha. He found that a Shunammite woman's son, (2 Kings 4:18-37) was raised by the prophet Elisha. Apparently, (2 Kings 13:20-21) Elisha was also connected with another in which a dead body was thrown on Elisha's bones and another man was brought back to life. The widow of Nain's son, (Luke 7:11-17) was the first of the resurrections that Jesus performed. There was also Jairus' daughter, (Luke 8:52-56) was a synagogue leader that Jesus brought back. The third person Jesus raised from the dead was Lazarus, (John 11). In Acts 9:36-43, Paul found Tabitha, (whose Greek name was Dorcas) lived in Joppa; she was resurrected by the Apostle Peter. Again, in Acts 20:7-12, Eutychus was dead and lived again by the Apostle Paul. Lastly, the Bible mentions resurrections that occurred in numbers when Christ was resurrected. He was sure there were Saints that throughout history have been recognized for their part in resurrecting people.

It was apparent that historically, the Bible mentioned people raising the dead; but modern society was not biblical. Paul thought for a second and paused to think of embalming, old and new methods for preparing the dead for burial; he was pretty sure no embalming fluid was pumped into bodies in ancient times…it could make it hard to bring a body back to life when it's filled with that crud.

Egyptian history mentioned some nasty things they did to bodies to mummify them but bringing a corpse back to life…that is surely sainthood in Catholicism. Although "St. Paul" had a ring to it, Paul was certain that he would appreciate Paul the Apostle telling him some advice right now. He was afraid to proceed, he was afraid to not…It was a damn "Catch-22".

Paul finally decided that he would not tempt fate, but if he were delivered unto this world to save the lives of others that God put in his path…then he would save them and damn the consequences!

The worst-case scenario, Paul figured, would be the Paparazzi, the media, and the naysayers; all of them ganging up on him for doing something right would be the worst that could happen. But Paul realized that it could impact the people at his work and the routine of helping animals too. It may even reach an ugly hand up towards his family or friends; but they all would realize that it's simply best to support Paul. He seemed to feel a little better about this now, maybe it's not as bad as he thought? He grabbed the single bottle of beer that had been in the fridge for about a month, twisting off the cap, he thought about adopting rules for using this "Healing".

Well, he thought, the number one thing that would tempt an earthly man upon the earth with a power of life and death; money. He thought as he scribbled down on a small post-note, "Number 1 – don't ever use it for money." Yes, he was quite proud of that one, it seemed to take away the greed of the world in using a power like this. Next, he thought it would be good to consider who to use it on, "Number 2" he scribbled; "don't ever use it on a bad or evil person." Yes, he was proud of that one as well, evil can beget evil. Why bring back an evil person to do more harm upon others. There should be a third rule, everything seems to come in threes, Paul thought. Maybe, "Number 3" he thought, should be more specific to him, "Don't ever use if he doesn't feel right or good about it. That seemed like a fair list, it allowed for Paul to have a personal say, but perhaps having a list would keep turmoil a little more controlled.

Paul liked having a list, he sipped at the beer, admiring his work, when the phone rang and jolted him so much he spilled beer on the carpet. He dabbed at the liquid, while grabbing at the phone. It was the darn Clinic calling again, "Hi Sir," the voice squeaked out, "it's Cara again," as if that made it all better. She advised him that a horse was down after breaking through a fence and eating alfalfa all night, the stomach was impacted, and the horse was down. Paul cussed under his breath when she said they couldn't contact Dr. Spencer. "It's a life or death situation," Cara pleaded over the phone, "It will probably die if you don't come!"

Paul got the address and headed out to handle the call, he set his half beer down, ate a handful of peanut candy to cloud his beer breath, and jumped into the rig to find a horse down. He stopped by the office to pick up a few items and to make sure he was ready for the proper patient. A horse is a large animal to help, he may need to restrain it to treat it. He also grabbed enough tranquilizer to put down a horse. His drive took him south of Bandon. He had a little trouble finding the place in the dark, but he finally saw some lights at the end of the long dirt driveway that he had turned left on from the highway.

Upon arriving, Paul found three vehicles all crowding most of the roadway, he pulled up and parked on the outside, (allowing an exit quickly if he needed to in a hurry.) He spotted Cara and couldn't understand why she would be at the site; she never reported to the actual emergency care site. He approached her, as if perhaps angry that she was there, "What are you doing here Cara?" Paul asked a bit too firmly.

"I'm sorry," Cara began to cry and apologize, "I just thought you might have trouble finding the place, and I wanted to know what we do to help animals," she blubbered.

"Whoa," Paul paused, raised his hands and placed them on her shoulders, "I'm so sorry, I must have come across like an asshole," Paul apologized, "it's terrific that you're here, I'll have to pay you overtime though, anytime we're called out." Paul now smiled and presented a better appearance to the girl, she obviously wasn't told by Paul not to report. She had apparently even gathered some supplies from the office for Paul too. He really felt bad that he snapped at her like that, he made a mental note to apologize more later.

"Let's go partner," Paul encouraged Cara, as she wiped a tear. "We have a horse to save," Paul said apologetically. The two of them headed for a nearby barn, they were met by a young, blond lady that must have been the owner.

"The horse is down, we had to load it on a wagon to get it into the barn," the alarmed owner of the animal spouted. She began talking about the animal, which is what Paul expected, it was time to get the people out of the way and for the professionals to take over. Paul knew he had to work fast, and a history story of a horse that he had no file on was not going to help. Paul cleared the area, he took vitals as Cara was writing frantically, to create a file on the horse that was apparently named, "Snip". Cara was drastically writing down apparent information to bill, etc. from the owner, which kept the woman off Paul. He could tell this Cara had skills.

Paul got out a couple I.V. packets, stapled them to the top of the wooden stall side that was available. He then placed a line into the animal's neck, grabbed the I.V. and connected the tube to get fluids into the animal. He then retrieved a bottle of glycerin and placed it next to the horse's mouth, he went into the bag and came out with a strange item that could have scared some folks. It was the false teat that you fed small calves' milk with, but in the light of the moon it looked sexual in nature. The two onlookers gazed at a peepshow that they probably would have paid money for in the city.

Paul then nippled the bottle of the thick and clear liquid in the bottle, the teat started to slip, but Paul forced it onto the bottle firmly. He then stuck it into the horse's mouth and held it up, making the clear ooze slide down the poor animal's throat. Next, he laughed as he pulled out a huge black dildo that would have served well in a damn porno movie! He looked over at Cara and swung the large dildo around his head. He plunged it into the poor rear of the horse and then energized the bunny! The horse began to move slightly, and Paul placed his body across it to hold it into place. Lastly, he injected something into the line, just as the two onlookers began to show even more interest in the pony show.

He now barked orders at the two that were just standing around gawking, "You two, get over here!" they awoke and sprang into action. "You, hold the horses halter tight, get ready to get the horse up when I tell you!" He looked at the other man and told him to open the corral gate, to prepare for the horse, "You will grab the lead, and then circle this corral with the horse walking until I leave!" The two understood their orders, and Paul asked the two ladies to step back. He pulled the line out quickly and slapped a prepared bandage over the small hole, he then kicked at the vibrator dildo as it entered the horse's rectal cavity! The horse jumped up, lifting the small man on the halter, it then walked a couple steps and then headed for the corral. The horse began a stream of poop that left a black moving dildo somewhere along the way. Paul picked up the magic tool, shook it and placed it into a large bag, zipped it, and threw it into his bag.

The owner of the horse and Cara were both laughing, the two men were chasing after the horse in the corral, Paul was getting his supplies, preparing to depart.

"You don't see that every day at the office," Cara tried not to laugh, "but it would have died if you hadn't interceded!"

"Thank you for recognizing that," Paul smirked, "it's not in all the books, it's old vet crap with a twist of porn!" Paul finished, looked around, and told Cara, "Please don't tell folks about some of this, they really can't understand the black dildo thing; it helps to excite the horse bowls, with some liquids and a shot of adrenaline, exercise now will save its life!"

Cara agreed, only because it would be an embarrassing tale, and it's hard to tell without mentioning the sight of that horse with a vibrating, black, dildo shaking as it ran for the corral. She wanted to not charge overtime, but Paul would not have it. He told her to document the emergency call – charging her overtime to the bill too. She understood that business is liable for her when she works, so she had to be on the clock. She asked Paul if she could do it again sometime, Paul agreed only if it was pre-authorized. No more surprises, that was the understanding. Cara thanked Paul and then the two exited and drifted home to their separate lives and houses.

Chapter 7

A couple of wonderfully enjoyable weeks of routine allowed Paul to rest up; things seemed to be going well at the office, he even got that darn garage floor that looked so terrible in his house painted with some gray specialty paint. It looked good. Paul liked completing things that could be seen, the little accomplishments that you can gauge, and be able to sit back and admire your work. As a vet, he usually got to see his work that brought comfort and care to animals; but somehow it seemed different. He thought about it for a while and soon came to the conclusion that the joy, fun, playing, healthy years of animals that were cared for wasn't seen by him. He hoped that the result of his care would bring the joy, but then he thought of the Fire Chief's dog, apparently biting a child. He didn't really mean to bring the dog back, he was just petting it in pity. Paul decided he had to be careful of what he touched.

He was getting ready to grab his keys and head out the door for work, when the phone rang. It was Cara, she had asked him to attend a special dedication ceremony at a new maritime museum after work. Paul wasn't sure about fraternization with employees, but he liked this refreshing assistant that wasn't afraid to get her hands dirty. She was about the only real woman in his life at the time, he didn't know much about her, so he stretched out of his comfort zone and asked if she would like to meet for dinner before the event. Cara surprised him and sprung at the opportunity, indicating her love of the seafood fettuccini at *Benetti's*. They agreed, and to keep it silent at the office.

Paul locked up and launched the bike, he had a swing in his step. He wasn't sure if it was the date, dame, or denial of his ability. He was just a regular guy going to work these past couple weeks. He loved the normality. After work, the two enjoyed the second tier of the restaurant with a nice view of the bay and ships. Paul and Cara each took their separate transportation, Paul didn't have much of a ride to the event, Cara arrived much sooner and did a quick make-up. As Paul slid up beside her car, she rolled the window down.

"Hi, sailor," Cara began, "New in town?"

Paul laughed, pulling a brochure out of his pocket, "If anyone sees us from work, I've been carrying this to say we're discussing some stuff from work."

Cara smiled, "Good thinking partner!" she thought to herself, "what a dweeb". She thought maybe the guy is a bit slow with girls, he's ignoring the flirty sailor routine. Cara instantly grabbed the hand that was resting on her vehicle window; holding the hand in place firmly. It initially frightened Paul, but then he thought it was romantic. "If we were going ten miles an hour forward, and I was holding on to your hand, could you keep up on your bike?"

"Well, I wouldn't…" Paul stalled, "I wouldn't put myself in that situation, that would invite an accident, I could be hurt, but yea, I guess I would just coast and steer."

"How about reverse?" Cara smiled, as she pulled the parked car into reverse with her foot upon the brake, the car jolted in place. She purposely gripped down on his hand, ensuring he couldn't remove it. She was surprisingly strong, and the car lurched backward almost two feet. "Okay partner," she grimaced, "give me a kiss or I'm going to gun it!"

Without thinking, Paul stretched inside the cab and kissed Cara firmly, thinking that if he didn't keep her engaged, her foot may slip off the brake again! Cara slammed the automatic into park, turned off the engine, and hugged into the kiss deeply. Paul was wondering what was going on, Cara grabbed the brochure from his hand and threw it into her back seat of the car. The two vehicles were touching, the two friends were becoming lovers. Paul thought that life couldn't get any better.

They attended the special dedication ceremony that included a beautiful lectern that had been constructed by the local correctional institution. The inmates had created a segment of a ship to fit the décor and the people accepted it graciously. The two decided on ice cream afterward to crown the evening off. It was a chance to ask what flavors each of them liked, it also gave each an excuse to continue the first date. As the two finally met up, (after Paul's eight block ride) they locked up the car and bicycle. Instantly, an old Oldsmobile barreled into the parking lot, it struck a small girl that had come out of a pizza parlor.

It happened so fast that the mother hadn't even caught the glimpse as she was still exiting the pizza place. Paul instinctively jumped into action since he was only one car length away! An elderly woman of large size rolled out of the driver's side door, she fell to her knees and began retching, amazed at what she had done! Paul got to the little toddler, but her poor little head was leaking into his hand as he held her, she was non-responsive. But Paul couldn't help feeling pity, hurt, pain, and his tears fell freely. He couldn't help it, he tried not to engage, he tried not to reveal himself, but it was useless.

A glimmer of light blue shimmer flashed, and the little girl started crying aloud. Real loud…she was screaming, "Mommy!" Paul picked her up to her feet, and she ran through the vomit, slipped and fell to the curb. Her mother now observing the small toddler fallen onto the curb, ran to her and picked her up, trying to comfort her, and stop her from crying. The elderly woman was still trying to stop heaving, but she wasn't sure what she had just seen, or *not*.

Regretfully Cara had front row seats to the show, and Paul turned to look at her and she was flabbergasted. "What the hell just happened?" she demanded from Paul. "You and I both saw that damn piece of shit car hit that little baby girl!" she pointed her finger at him.

"Okay, okay," Paul took a big visible breath, held it and then exhaled, "we can't talk about this here, please follow me to my place and I'll discuss this with you, Cara!"

"Skip the ice cream," Cara laughed, "this is going to be good…I can't wait for you to explain this!"

Paul mounted the bike like a kid going home to get spanked, everything was going so well, he thought. As he gauged the traffic as a responsible cyclist should, he headed home, peddling slowly on purpose. He had to come up with something to tell her; he dreaded it all the way on the journey home. Cara couldn't race ahead like she had been doing; she had to drive at the pace Paul was going, she had no idea where he lived. As Paul arrived, locked up the bike, and took off his helmet; Cara locked the car and launched towards the door that Paul was unlocking. She had been thinking all the way to the house, but she still couldn't explain what she had seen.

Paul threw some clothes out of the way, and Cara took a seat on the recently cleared couch. The two were coasting in the past, toward possible romance; Paul felt like his stomach was about to empty in front of her. He wasn't sure himself, he wasn't certain about the ramifications of telling anyone about this. There would be uncertainty, doubt, and surely fear; Paul feared the conversation that would need to follow. He thought for a second that maybe it would be good to unload his monkey off his back by telling someone.

"This is going to sound absurd, as a professional Veterinarian, a Christian man, and a believer in science; but everything I'm about to tell you," Paul paused, "is true." Paul swallowed nothing in his throat hard, "Please hold questions and interruptions, because I may not be able to tell this tale twice."

"Okay," Cara agreed, "but I'm not leaving until I get some hard answers," she then thought about being in his house and what she had said, "wait a minute, that sounded bad…"

Paul interrupted her and said, "You will have your answers. Do you remember when I was flown out to that cruise ship, well I was kind of trapped inside a protective chamber and suit, when the Birdfire epidemic hit. All I know, is that I somehow was infected like everyone else. In turn, I think something happened to give me some gift of healing people. I didn't want anyone to see it, but you saw what happened." Paul winced in pain for a second, his abdomen was wrenching, and it was a sharp, stabbing pain that passed quickly. Cara picked up on it quickly, she was a very observant person.

"Hey, are you okay Paul?" she asked, reaching forward, as if to catch him if he were to double over on the couch.

"Yes, I'm fine, it's all this excitement, and maybe seafood shuffling around," Paul lied. He was beginning to recollect more of the past and the temporary sensation that followed the Healing. The pain did pass, but it appeared to be a bit more intense than before, Paul would take an ibuprofen or two later. "So, I really need you to keep this to yourself," Paul pleaded, "I'm afraid of the consequences if it got out." Paul reached over and grabbed Cara's hand genuinely and lovingly.

"Of course, Paul," Cara confirmed. "It's one of those things that people wouldn't believe, if they didn't see it themselves." Cara smiled warmly, "But you have to promise me that if you become ill, hurt, or just need someone…" she leaned over and kissed him, "you'll call me."

"Thank you, Cara," Paul said, (only because he wanted a reason to kiss her back again). He kissed her for a few seconds, it was followed by his hand gently touching her cheek, she liked it. "I'm probably not the most romantic guy," Paul admitted, "but you have to admit I sure know how to show a girl a heck of time!" Paul got her to admit that she didn't anticipate a date like this one, (and she wasn't sure that she ever wanted another crazy one like this soon.) She seemed to put all the questions on recess because it was getting late, and Paul knew he didn't have all the answers anyway. It wouldn't help to tell her about the past use of the ability, he thought; but he did feel like someone on his side could come in handy. Cara was a blessing.

Paul wondered about the little toddler, the little girl must have jetted out ahead of her mother at the pizza joint, probably excited about getting home to birthday presents or something. She didn't see that Old's coming; but her mother did see her on the curb afterward. Paul then wondered about the driver of the vehicle. There was vomit and probably blood and body fluids; but would anyone admit to a hit and run, that didn't have a victim? It may get shuffled off, but he would ask around the office and check the newspaper to see if there were any police dispatched.

Paul wondered what the little toddler would have told her mother? The poor kid probably doesn't understand or know what happened herself. One minute she's getting pizza with mom, and then next…she's under the front of an Oldsmobile. Paul remembered holding her little head in his palm, supporting the head of a lifeless child. He had felt a shallow, empty, hole, that seemed a bit overwhelming; as if it were the girl's lifeforce. Paul wanted to bring a fullness, a spark of hope and life into the vague translucence.

Something within the center of Paul had welled-up, a fountain of life had sprung forth, it had filled him; and then overflowed into the small vessel, and she came falling back into the body, that Paul held dearly. If bringing the little girl back to life filled Paul with such love and compassion that he could not measure; what had the small child felt?

There was no darn handbook, no one to ask questions, (Paul would love to phone a friend on this stuff). He didn't know how it worked, Paul believed it was not for him; a simple earthly man, to understand the powers that very few men in history wielded. He didn't know if this was a gift from God, but he would treat it so. If there were a Muslim that were saved by Paul…he decided that maybe Muhammed can work a deal with God; or Buddha, or Jehovah, or any other worshipped name. "Yup," Paul caught himself thinking aloud, "I'm multi-denominational!"

It still seemed like a good idea to keep the whole thing under wraps, he would only entrust Cara; besides she was sweet and wonderful, and he liked her. But Paul was no fool, he believed there may still be a lot to learn about this Healing. He wasn't sure what the public or press would do if they were to be enlightened by observing Paul save someone. It seemed like the average person could guess what might happen:

Science would want to perform an autopsy to find out what makes him tick; religious leaders would want to know what fueled his fire; and most likely, money would want to buy it. Regretfully, the world lightning-fast communication around the world – would want to talk about it, investigate and report; and the public would want to say they knew him personally. This was the world he lived in today. Maybe these standards were around since time began, (except the lightning communication). Paul imagined in biblical days of when apostles walked the earth, alchemists would want to know how it was done, and there were those thirty pieces of silver. Instead of Romans wanting to take his head, he would have psychologists wanting to take what was in his head. It may be impossible to keep the whole thing a secret, but Paul was determined to try to keep it as long as possible.

Lastly, Paul thought about discussing this with his parents; but then he quickly decided that "plausible denial" would be best, so he wouldn't bring it up to them either. Besides, how in the world would he describe this to his parents anyway? He wasn't sure that he could describe this, he had difficulty describing it to Cara. There was still a lot more to learn before he could precisely explain it, or control it, or simply ignore it.

He would need to add a fourth rule to his list; be careful not to bring life back into animals, (that darn dog thing seemed to go terribly bad) and he would be very careful about bringing the dead back to life. But if God laid a victim in his path, and he felt it met the tests that he had thought up, he would need to use the gift, (even if it meant discovery).

The little girl, he decided; probably didn't know what happen, nor would she be able to communicate what she experienced. He would just hope that time would pass, and the small girl would make good use of the new life that had been blessed within her. Paul was proud of himself for at least being able to say that he saved her life…he then realized that pride was a deadly sin as well. He bowed his head and prayed to remain humble.

Paul asked the blessing, and then ate a bite; he watched some television news to see if there was anything out there, cooking in the public eye. Nothing – was probably good, he thought. He then rejoiced in the little girl and her new opportunities that would present themselves to her as he went to bed. His nightly prayers would continue to begin with him thanking God for the blessing of The Healing. That evening Paul spent more time in his prayers for the little girl. He wished that he could do more for her; he had a haunting feeling that perhaps he had done more…he just didn't know it.

Chapter 8

The next day was filled with delight. He didn't hear any buzz around town or the office about a small girl rescued, or a man admitted to psychiatric care in bizarre accident with his Oldsmobile. Cara seemed cool. She didn't act differently, no presumptions, no "Hey, what about that date…huh?" or any other visible flirtations. The two seemed to be playing it cool, and Paul liked it. He went about his day, finding the standard routine very boring and satisfying. Paul was a bit surprised when at the end of the day, he was the last one there, answering to some group of women's voices, all yelling in unison, "You got the lock-up Doctor Baldwin?"

Answering the gals to confirm him closing the office; Paul was a little disappointed that Cara didn't loiter for just a bit. He sighed heavily, then began the mental checklist of closing and locking of meds, ensuring doors were secured, and computers on stand-by for emergencies. He heard the door in the front open and close, causing him to briefly look up. It was Cara!

She came in and through the waiting area quickly, she reached inside her blouse and pulled out a brilliant colored scarf; as she semi-whispered, "I told them I forgot my scarf – isn't this fun!" She asked the rhetorical question, but as she pulled her scarf, the scent of innocence and bubble gum combined into an intoxicant in his head. She smiled widely, grabbed his head with both hands, pulled him close and kissed him deeply. "That will have to do for now," she smiled again, "isn't this fun, I just love secrets; and I'm good at keeping them too!"

Paul was overwhelmed with the battery of colors, the intoxicating smile, and that darn bubble gum mixed with "fleur de' yummy". The kiss was over the top! Paul wasn't a big romantic, but he literally felt his heart flutter. He almost forgot what he was doing, the checklist went out the door about three seconds ago. Paul had frozen, he was trying to think, for three or four seconds he wasn't sure what his next move would or should be. Women are so confusing, all he knew was he wanted to buy some bubble gum immediately.

Paul locked everything and headed out the door; mounted his bike and it seemed like only seconds later, found himself home. He didn't remember the crosswalks, the traffic, or even the hill. He had somehow drifted home on the bicycle without an accident. He locked it up and unlocked the house, happy with the day. Paul thought his life was maybe finally on cruise control, he was noticing the trees, the ferns everywhere, and the colors of the hillside; dotted with houses, filled with loving families.

He seemed to find himself cleaning up the house, he got the laundry started, dishes unloaded from the dishwasher, and even ran the vacuum for a bit. He stopped – suddenly, he had caught himself humming "*A Spoon Full of Sugar*" and he had to laugh at himself. The knock on the door was both surprising and invited, he floated to the door to find Cara in casual attire. She had parked her bike next to Paul's. She was doing that thing with her smile again, Paul didn't invite her in, she just pushed him through the doorway! Paul was happy to see she closed the door behind her, when he noticed it she laughed aloud.

"Oh, I see," Cara began, "thought I was born in a barn, did you?" "Can you believe," she smiled widely again, "that I peddled my ass all the way over here, leaving my car at home!" She began to explain that they would need to not be parking cars at each other's place.

"Come in," Paul said jokingly. He smiled back again, "I got the joke too…you know, the peddling of ass." Paul saw her return the smile. Paul grabbed her hand, "Listen, I probably won't be able to recite this speech to you like I rehearsed, but I'll try to get this out in one shot," he maintained eye contact with her. "For a boss to date an employee, is complicated at best; for a guy with some crazy unknown ability to date anyone, has got to be complicated," Paul explained. "I'm about to throw something else into the equation that will complicate the heck out of it."

"Oh God, you're gay, or LGBT or some other alphabet!" Cara exclaimed, interrupting.

"No," Paul regained control of the conversation, "I'm a Christian virgin!" He recoiled a bit, allowing their hands to break apart, "There, I've said it, you can laugh; you're not going to get lucky tonight…sorry."

Cara grinned, "Silly," she began, "I'm not a virgin, but I wish I would have waited." She again approached him and took his hand, "I'm really not as fast as you think," she pulled a tissue from her bra like a magician, dabbing at a tear, she sniffled, "I'm all show and no go!"

Paul embraced her and wiped a tear away from her eye, "I have been high all afternoon since you kissed me in the office today!" "You," he caressed her cheek, "are all that I can think about, you're in my head and heart!"

"Oh, I can wait for you, I'm in no hurry Paul," Cara smiled, "I'm still going to be flirting with you, I like to see you light up!" She told Paul how she liked a guy with manners and religious background, and then she said something that was odd. She said that Paul had an "old soul" and he didn't know what to make of it. He had remembered something that his grandmother had told him about old souls once.

Cara reminded Paul that she was the only person he could rely upon to keep his secret, they even pinky-swore and oath, (which seemed childishly fun to Paul.) After the secret oath, the two laughed and Cara kissed Paul, they agreed to keep the secret, but also the kindled romance too. The two seemed delighted with each other, Paul found Cara gave him purpose.

"Okay, stud," Cara moved about like a jungle animal, "I'm headed home, but you can't believe what I'm going to be thinking about tonight!" Paul blushed and escorted her to the door, (before he could reconsider her exit). She was exciting, unpredictable, and very addicting, and it was just what the animal doctor ordered.

It was early, so Paul grabbed a bite of leftovers and headed out to his bike, he really was a bit too close to that ice cream shop for a diet to succeed. The amaretto pistachio was to die for, so he would often grab a single dip as a treat. He couldn't help but think of Cara along the way, he was going to have to introduce her to the single dip that couldn't be beat. Upon arrival, he saw a teenage boy that was just sitting on his bike, parked in the front of the pizza joint. As Paul rode up near the ice cream parlor, the boy sprang into life and peddled over to meet up with Paul. The two didn't know each other by name, Paul hadn't ever met the kid, but he seemed to act as though he knew Paul. Stopping abruptly, sliding off the seat to his feet, straddling the bike, this young teenage boy started a conversation:

"Hey, sir," the teenager began, "were you here recently, did you see an old man in a crappy car hit a little girl?"

"I'm just here for the ice cream," Paul responded. "Not sure what you're talking about," Paul lied.

"Well, my little sister was bumped by a car here," the teenager reengaged. "If you are the guy, my sister wanted to thank you." The teenage boy began to cry uncontrollably, "She told me to come here and wait to talk to any guy riding a bike for ice cream at this time of night."

"Hey, are you okay?" Paul began to be concerned, it seemed uncharacteristic for the kid to cry in front of a perfect stranger. "Do you need to call someone, I have a cell phone," Paul tried to console the kid.

"I'm okay," the kid wiped a tear, "thanks to my sister." He looked into Paul's eyes, "You see this kid at school had been beating on me, so I got home and grabbed the gun out of my dad's closet…" The story stopped, as if the kid was deciding whether to tell the tale or not. "I wasn't going to kill anyone, I was just going to scare him with it, so he would pick on me anymore," the kid seemed to be unloading on Paul. "I took the thing out of the bottom that holds the bullets, so it couldn't hurt anyone." The story stopped again, until Paul encouraged the teller to finish the tale. "Well," he swallowed hard, "I was learning how to point the gun and Katrina came in and grabbed the gun, I told her it was unloaded, and I was going to pull the trigger at her, when she screamed and hit the gun and it went off!" He stopped and lowered his head, breaking the stare that had held Paul's eyes fixed. "I would have killed her, there was a bullet still in the gun!" he broke down on the curb. His bicycle fell in the opposite direction, the kid was crying, probably glad to simply confess to someone.

Paul consoled him and let him know that he could call his parents to have someone pick him up; but the kid was not wanting anyone that knew him to see him in the condition he was in. Paul wanted so much to admit to the boy that he was the one, but it wouldn't make any difference now, and he really needed to remain anonymous. Paul introduced himself to Ronnie, he gave him one of his business cards and let him know that he could contact Paul anytime and he would try to come to his aid. Ronnie thanked him and apologized for the outpouring, but Paul understood more than Ronnie would ever know. Paul reminded him that his sister was a blessing, and that he should never take her for granted. He went in and got a couple cones to share and the two cyclists parted.

It was a strange meeting, but lately Paul wasn't too surprised at what seemed strange. He was almost getting a bit "gun-shy" with who to touch, what not to touch, watching out for the public, sneaking a kiss with Cara, and now serving almost as a priest listening to a poor teenage boy confess.

It was a bit surprising when Cara asked Paul to attend church with her. Not because they were looking at nuptials, it was more exploring each other to know a bit more about themselves. Cara went to Paul's church with him equally, they weren't shopping, as much as looking for a mix of what each other liked. Paul was baptized as a Lutheran, Cara was a bit of a Baptist; and they kind of found the time together was special to them, but they were seen by some people as a bit of a blossoming couple that was very private.

The next few weeks were filled with fun and frolic, Cara was more than often; unpredictable. She would do these crazy stunts at work, surprise Paul with exotic attempts at dinner, and she appeared to be able to pull his humor out of the box. She was certainly testing Paul's incorrigible and reliable pattern that was borderline Obsessive-Compulsive Disorder. Paul almost looked forward to the next "surprise" that she would throw like a curveball; you never knew what to expect.

Paul found the black dildo that he had used on the horse when the two of them saved it – in a baggie with the tip cut off; under his pillow when he woke the morning after watching a godfather movie with Cara the night before. It was classic Cara, Paul laughed as he flung the baggie and missile toward the garbage in the bathroom. He decided that he wouldn't ask her if that "tool" from his kit was going to be replaced.

She liked to pull the pin on a grenade and then wait to see what happens next. Paul got to work the next morning and found a special five-foot tall poster of how to care for your horse outside the lobby. But then there was the very small and single purple violet that was stuck in his keyhole when he got home. It boggled his mind how she could be so many places and do so much without being seen. He was finding her to be more than entertaining, she was fun and exciting! Cara hadn't brought up "the Healing" incident; and Paul liked that. No news certainly appeared to be good news when it came to the subject.

Cara had to volunteer at the cat-house shelter too; she was really very helpful in dealing with some of the more challenging cats that were a bit mean from being abused. Paul thought it would be best not to mention Mrs. Johnson's passing to Cara. There was a new lady that was taking charge of the donated house full of cats. Paul thought it might be a good time to get even with the little vixen; as they drove to the house, he was rubbing catnip on Cara's coat. He thought this would be entertaining. Paul entered the house first, clearing the way as they could; but the catnip caused a total cat-a-strophe; the constant bombardment on Cara finally squeezed out – slamming the door behind her. She used some colorful language that the new lady was quite taken back! Paul looked at the grenade-puller through the window of the door and without saying a word…he lipped the word, "catnip" silently…hoping not to set off thunder inside the house again; if the cats knew the word. Paul pointed to jacket and Cara finally put the puzzle together; smiling…she threatened to get even. At least she was smiling; Paul thought.

Mrs. Nichols, (the new caretaker of the house) asked if maybe the veterinary doctor be the only one that assisted; Paul had to repair the fences that he had destroyed with the stunt. Cara took off; walking down the hill, abandoning Paul to his cat-house. It was more than funny however for Paul to see two or three cats following her down the hill; it took her a while to see them. She tried a few times to get them to leave her alone, until she finally resorted to outright running. Paul advised Mrs. Nichols that he would need to be rapping up early and make another house-call. It was a bit of a lie; since he meant his own house. He was now fearing the retaliation factor that Cara could produce.

Cara met Paul at his door, announcing that she was borrowing his clothes washer and she was going to stay until the darn thing got dry too. Paul knew better than to argue, so he simply asked if she would like some Chinese food take-out for the evening – hoping to mend the fence. She agreed, but just as Paul was closing the door behind him; he overheard Cara yell, "And no catnip!"

Paul snickered as he got in his pick-up truck, he finally got one on the little pixie! It would serve her right; after all the tricks, she pulled over the past weeks on him. He dropped by his favorite of the many restaurants in the area. He loved the bar-b-que pork, it was slightly warmed, tender, and had that red hoisin sauce color on the outside. Everyone in the area had their favorite, but the area seemed blessed with quite a variety. Grabbing the order after a brief fifteen-minute wait that urged him to call Cara on her cell – just to disrupt whatever trap she was plotting at the house.

He finally got back to the house with the warm, delicious smelling, to go bags; and entered the house. He didn't see Cara anywhere, it was scary, but also curious at the same time. He yelled her name and she jumped out from the closet, she fell to one knee and said, "Paul will you marry me?" She was proposing to him! Paul wondered if she knew the rules to this game, and this wasn't funny. He gazed into her eyes and a tear formed, Paul was taking too long; it became an uncomfortable silence; Paul finally broke the silence by telling her he would love to marry her.

"You were thinking pretty hard about it," Cara said worryingly, "are you sure you want to commit to an answer today?"

"Absolutely," Paul said gallantly, "It was "the Healing" that had me worried for a second, I can't promise that it won't be a problem in the future, honestly; it definitely will."

Chapter 9

The two young lovers decided not to tell anyone just yet, they would shop for a ring, (which incidentally, means the woman picks and the man pays.) Paul and Cara were in no real hurry, but they did manage to break free and spend time with each other over the next few weeks. Paul planned on introducing Cara to his family in Eastern Oregon; he worked up a good schedule to implement some covert moves too. Cara was going to take vacation and talk a lot about her just spending it with family. In this case, it would be Paul's, but it could count for future family plans too. Paul was honest in telling his partner that he needed to take time off and he would be going home to see family, (so he couldn't be called upon for emergencies locally.)

Paul had contacted his parents in a small town near John Day, Oregon. They would be excited to meet this pretty assistant that he had been talking about for a few months. There was always some hidden mystique about Seneca, the small town that had come to the aid of Paul's family, years ago when he was young. Paul decided not to go into historical detail with Cara, it was enough for her to know that his parents loved the small town and would defend it, if need be. It was always wonderful to go to the mountains, the trees, some snow-capped ridgelines, and usually a few small waterfalls that have iced over along the way.

The big question on Cara's mind, wasn't really related to her meeting Paul's family; she wanted to know if he had told them of his wonderful God-given gift? She asked if there was anything they could or shouldn't discuss in the car as they drove; she was clever like that. Paul fell for the trap, and she immediately brought up the subject. Paul let her know that he wouldn't be talking about it and hadn't briefed his parents yet. Cara asked if they were religious, since he was baptized a Lutheran. Paul advised her that they were initially from the Bible-belt of Nebraska before Oregon, and they certainly were strong-willed Christians.

After an exhaustive trip, they finally got there, and Paul introduced Cara to his parents. They all had a nice dinner, (after grace) and they each got bundled in to their separate rooms; after a kiss goodnight. Paul's mother asked if they would be attending church with them around eleven in the morning, he agreed to go and accepted the invitation on behalf of Cara, Paul's mother gave him advice, "Honey, never take for granted what a woman wants to be asked."

His mom wouldn't let him go up and ask her though, it seemed like a double standard, but he knew he wasn't going anywhere near her bedroom under his parent's roof. He and Cara had messed around, but they hadn't taken the pre-marital plunge yet. Cara was wanting to, but Paul was still not sure, especially with the looming ability to play Lazarus. He would play it safe and lay low on all accounts. He would pick his own time to reveal his secrets.

The morning brought a large breakfast and a few more introductions of family and friends of family, to Cara. She wasn't all that great with names but figured she may have some time to get to know them later. Everyone seemed to be getting ready for church, so Cara grabbed some less casual items, but she didn't come to dress-up and impress anyone, all her pretty outfits were back home. She asked Paul if she looked okay, but it was like asking a rhetorical question.

Paul wasn't all dressed up either, this wasn't a gussied-up church, from what Cara could gather. They took a few different vehicles, to spread the family out, Paul and Cara decided they should take their vehicle together. They all landed safely in the pews, Paul introduced Cara to the pastor. His name was German and hard to spell, but as kids everyone just called him, "Pastor Shootie" but Paul was certain there were some other silent consonants hiding in his real spelling. He was delighted to meet Cara, as one would expect, he welcomed her and looked forward to seeing more of her.

The service went just as predicted, (the planned hymns pages on the wall) until they got to the holy sacrament. Paul asked Cara if she wanted to attend, half-way apologizing for springing it on her – she declined, but Paul went with his mother and father up to kneel. When the Pastor bent slightly forward to bring the small silver saucer of bread to the recipient…he just kept going! He fell right there on the alter, forward and still tumbling over everyone in front of him.

The holy man was reeling toward heaven at a speed only light could compete, trumpets sounding, a blast of white billowing clouds separated, and he was meeting St. Peter at the golden gates as he had always imagined. He fell to his knees, as an unworthy man – unknowing that he had already been judged and was helped to his (now) sandaled feet. As he approached the gate, there was a pause and a wonderfully loving voice advised that he was not done.

The entire congregation was flabbergasted, someone yelled to call 911; but the Pastor had no pulse, no breath, and no AED in the small church. Dr. Collins was in the congregation and he began CPR, barking orders for others to follow. The ambulance would be twenty-five minutes out, everyone one knew that was the quickest time recorded. Pastor Shootie would be doing exactly what he wanted to do, when he died. If he could have asked for a specific death, this would have been it. He was preaching God's word, he was giving the communion, this would be a tremendous way to leave this world!

Cara looked at Paul, he was sitting on the bench now, still in shock like everyone else. Minutes passed like high-speed cars on the freeway, without anyone being able to do much. Cara didn't know the rules for use of "the Healing but it didn't matter, Paul had been rifling the rules that he had developed through his head! He grabbed the exhausted doctor that had given up on the CPR now and was instinctively looking at his watch to call it. Paul flung the doctor back and lunged on top of Pastor Shootie, he then placed his hand on the dead man's chest and began praying silently. Although you could hear a hair drop, only tears fell. Within a split second – Pastor Shootie exclaimed, "Wait!" he repeated it several times as he sat upright. The entire congregation that had been flabbergasted before; was now in awe!

The doctor reeled back from his fall to approach Paul, but when he saw the holy man being helped to his feet by several people in amazement; the doctor began to cry. A woman yelled the obvious, that this was a miracle. Paul and Cara knew exactly what kind of miracle they had witnessed before. Paul was thinking all the rules about no money, no bad or evil, and he certainly felt it was right to do "the Healing."

There were approximately sixty witnesses to the event, many had their cellphones out, taking pictures afterwards, making personal statements of what they perceived or thought they saw. The entire "lay-low" plan was shot to hell – or heaven, Paul didn't know but his parents sprang into action, telling everyone that this was to be held close and they didn't want all the publicity – and neither did the town. Several people agreed loudly, saying something to the effect of protect the healer! Whatever it was, Paul liked the idea that maybe it wouldn't spread like wildfire.

Paul and Cara were almost silent on the way back to his parent's house. At least Paul didn't have to explain it to her, that was a relief for a few minutes. Paul winced in pain briefly, holding his side; it passed, and he took his hand quickly away from his side and reached for Cara's. The two held hands while he drove to the house trying to figure out how he would explain this. Paul shoved the rig into park, he stared deeply into Cara's eyes, "If I ever have to get the hell out of Dodge, I will need for you to come here…without any questions, no matter what you do; you must promise me!"

"Why…why would you ever want me to do that, you mean leave you and flee to here?" Cara sobbed. "What would make you say that," Cara tried again, "if I'm your wife, I will stand by your side!"

"Yea, I know," Paul tried to explain, "Till death do you part," he agreed. "But…" he paused, "if I knew you were in danger, and I asked you to do it; you would for me, wouldn't you?"

"Well, I suppose," Cara thought on it, "only if you would be safe; and both our safety depended on it, I guess."

"That would be the only time and reason for me to ask this of you, Cara," Paul smiled warmly, knowing that it was Cara's weakness. "You know I love you," Paul padded the bet.

"Okay, if I ever say meet me at the synagogue, you'll know it means head to Seneca!" Paul nodded, getting her to nod too. "Neither of us are Jewish, so it would be easy to understand to only us," Paul plotted.

"You're not going to get all full of yourself, are you?" Cara smiled, "don't go secret agent and crap on me!"

The two lovers exited the vehicle to enter the house, with parents and family waiting for them to answer a barrage of questions. As they both simultaneously closed the vehicle doors, Cara gave that look at Paul, "You better have some answers buddy!"

As Paul reached for the door knob to open, his mother opened the door to greet them, she hugged him as only a mother could; but there was something distinctly different this time. She began to sob, oblivious to the worlds peering eyes. She pulled back away from her baby for a moment, to gaze deep into his soul via his eyes. Paul knew this feeling, it reminded him when his brother had cut the whiskers off "Maggie" the cat; and then hidden the shears under the bed. It probably didn't help matters to self-admit, "I didn't cut Maggie whiskers and put the skissors under the bed."

"I knew you were blessed with a gift, because your brother had been blessed before you; but you were young then," his mother admitted. She looked at the family gathered around the living room; they all seem to be in on it, smiling and nodding in a positive manner.

"Well, why didn't someone tell me about this, why am I the last one to know?" Paul asked, without mentioning the cruise ship containment, and the Bird Fire.

Paul's father stood up, facing his son, he smiled, "If I promised you a new car when you graduated, and then didn't deliver, what would you think son?" This brought an enlightened laughter from Paul, Cara began laughing, (not sure what the joke was at first.)

Paul learned a fragment of the secrets and a lot of the protection that was Seneca, Oregon. It had some mystical appeal that seemed to have blossomed into a true and functional Sanctuary for gifted or fugitive folks. Cara listened intently, semi-believing in parts and pieces of stories.

Paul and Cara were assured by everyone that they would be monitoring and discrediting anything that may have been seen regarding the Healing of Pastor Shootie. It was certain that someone probably will eventually think they are doing good – and would blast the image on the damn internet. Hopefully with a gaggle of Senecans tagging everything and claiming altered video; the matter may dissolve and never catch up the young lovers.

The ride home seemed to be filled with hundreds of questions from Cara, she had all kinds of "what if?" and "maybe you could" Paul started throwing a bit of reality back to get her to laugh, "What if we had sex and my love-making turned you into a frog!" Paul got her to giggling, he knew after that, it was all down-hill. Paul had her non-stop giggling. He loaded up another round, closed the breach, and then grabbed the trigger, ready to squeeze another giggle out of her for at least a few minutes' worth. He fired away, "What if we have sex, and my love turned you into gifted for rubbing against me?"

Silence fell over the vehicle, the only thing making any noise was the road and where the rubber met the road. They hadn't ever considered what impact this could have on Cara, or even her child in the future, (if there was one now.)

"Well, it's quiet enough for some music I think," Cara smiled as she turned on the CD player. It didn't matter what was playing, both young lovers were thinking about each other and what the future may hold. It is one thing to have commitment, but it's not a bond broken by a piece of divorce paperwork. The two cruised the long trip back to the coast, enjoying the stops and sights along the way. They both had a lot to consider, but it would not impact their feelings for each other, nor the trip that seemed to unite them even stronger. Timing seemed to have a lot to do with it. Paul wondered what Pastor Shootie thought about divine intervention; as a man of God, he probably is counting his blessings, loving life and his family. Paul wasn't sure if it was fortunate that he was there to bring him back or being placed there to carry out some big plan and God's will. One thing was for sure, the church still had a leader.

The elderly pastor awoke from a peaceful slumber that his wife referred to as a nap. He said he felt renewed, he didn't have those previously untraceable aches, and his brief memory loss was purloined somehow. He walked over to his wife and kneeled, without care for his previous injurious joints. He told her they needed to pray and thank God for this blessing, his wife reminded him of the previous nine prayers, thanking him; but added one, for an even ten.

The pastor smiled afterward, he semi-laughed, "it's going to be hard to focus writing a service to people without curving into the Bible's recollection of people being brought back to life." He told his wife that he would agree to speak of being thankful, versus the resurrecting; but it would be difficult.

Kellie Montrose saw the small neighborhood hoodlum fall from the crappy bunch of scraps that were nailed together; a poor excuse for a treehouse that was over twenty feet high. "The guy was a bully, it served him right," the little toddler thought to herself. She was going to start laughing, as soon as the bully got up and started crying about a broken something.

But he didn't get up. He wasn't moving. He sounded like a big sack of potatoes, thudding, when he hit. There was a big bellow that had ghastly exhaled when he hit too. Still not getting up. Still not moving.

Kellie went over the pale bully, once threatening; he now looked harmless, almost worth saving. She had taken CPR with her daddy in her preschool, she could also spell almost a hundred words! She placed her ear over the bully's mouth…nothing. She took the biggest breath she could muster, she did the head-tilt, nose pinched, and seal on the nasty's mouth. She exhaled and repeated, the young bastard began coughing; and Kellie just ran away.

She was afraid that he might hurt her; he once put a spider on Mollie Wiggins! She also thought her mommy would be asking why she was down this far from the house. She didn't want to endanger any future Birthday pizza!

Chapter 10

The trip from Eastern Oregon to the Western provided bountiful views and change in climate; just as Eastern Washington varied from the Western region. The hot high-desert is very cold in the winter; Eastern Oregon and Washington had less timber. But the Western sides of both states had more rain and moderate temperatures, resulting in timber, and even more timber. Paul and Cara enjoyed the scenery, but Paul mostly enjoyed finding spots to stop and take in some sights without discussing much about The Healing. He needed a brief recess, and the incredible Stonehenge was a great stop near the Mary Hill Mansion and Winery.

With the rolling Columbia River dividing the two states, it demands respect. The sheer vastness and size, (only harnessed by multiple large dams) the Columbia provides a perfect location to view Stonehenge. It was identical to the English, historical marvel; but it stands strong against the high winds; and dampness in the decaying sister that is found in Salisbury, England. The youthful and strong sister lies on the Washington side and is a unique for any photo with the stately, tall, perfect pillars circling everyone's interest.

Paul once saw a group of wedding photos done exclusively at the Stonehenge. Bridesmaids were popping out from behind pillars, the couple laying on a mock "death-slab" sacrifice table in the center. It was cool, but a bit bizarre too. Paul invited Cara to sit briefly on the rock table, after the last group of two families returned to their vehicles. The brief solitude would be lost in a few minutes, many people arrived, took a photograph and stole a memory that would be discussed at some dinner or family visit.

Paul patted the stone as though it were comfortable, inviting her to sit next to him. Cara smiled that curious, but inviting interest, smile as though she were a cat. She prowled around Paul and approached him from the other, opposite side, and jumped up from behind him, landing beside him.

"Okay, how about honest answers to any question you have?" Paul blurted out the offer. He wasn't sure what she would ask, there could be entirely different things on her mind. She may ask his marital intentions, The Healing, or just what she might want to stop and have dinner.

"Are you ready for questions," Cara began, "that you may not be prepared to answer?" She smiled widely again, "I know the old saying…don't ask what you don't want to know." She grabbed his hand, "I only have one question, Paul."

"No one is here, ask away, I can take it," Paul laughed nervously.

"When you use this gift, The Healing; or resurrection; does it hurt you afterward?" Cara looked concerned. "I noticed after Pastor Shootee, you grimaced in a bit of pain afterward," she admitted to Paul.

"Wow," Paul responded, "that isn't any of the questions I thought you would ask." Paul repositioned himself on the rock edge, "To tell the truth, I guess I did have a bit of pain, but it was like a subsided quickly spasm," Paul was glad she asked a caring question. He pulled her close and they shared an embrace and a kiss for a full minute or more. Paul told her not to worry about that yet, he felt fine. But he did promise to let her know if he ever was in great pain because of The Healing, he would tell her. They seemed like perfectly matched, young lovers, trying to figure things out, while dealing with something that no one had seen in thousands of years.

Their trip landed them back in Coos Bay at night, it was nice to get back to some comfort of home. Cara had things to get done at her place, so Paul dropped her off and headed back to his house. Paul got unloaded and nestled into home, he was almost afraid to turn on the computer or check emails. Logging onto his emails, Paul was busy deleting junk mail, when his cell phone blipped to indicate a new message. It was the message from Cara advising she was fine and had a great trip with Paul. He felt a warm, cuddly, and heartfelt feeling coming over him that seemed to pull a tear. As he wiped the tear away, he seemed to feel convicted to love for the special person that could understand him for the rest of his life. He would treasure this feeling, hoping that he could perhaps, someday describe the feeling to Cara; he wondered if mere words could even be found to describe it. Paul believed it was somehow – meant to be.

The glow he was experiencing collapsed with another message from the Sheriff of Coos County, they advised Paul that his partner couldn't be reached; they needed the Veterinarian Clinic for a make-shift triage for bodies recovered from a crab boat that had been hit by squall, when the ship was tried to cross the bar. The shoal capsized the craft, killing all aboard;

the clinic was close enough to stack and identify the crew being gathered at the time. It was a heart-pounding of another type that Paul had as he quickly texted he was on his way to rendezvous with the Sheriff.

The office lights reminded Paul that he was still supposed to be unavailable and off until the following day. As he made the quick route through the office and treatment areas, he heard Sheriff Wright, yelling Paul's name. He extended all the treatment areas, (to take on the largest of pets – or pieces of human bodies apparently.) The Sheriff used some expletives Paul hadn't heard for a while, "And the whole thing is just a damn nightmare…"

Paul agreed, and then informed the Sheriff that he had only just gotten home from a trip and was supposed to be off until the following day. "What do we know about the condition of the bodies?" Paul asked, "how many should I expect?"

"Apparently, there were eight aboard, so I'd plan for the worst Doc," Sheriff Wright recommended. "We will need to get the complete list from the company for matching pay records to verify, but sometimes the Oregon Coast gets a shark or Orca, chasing after the seals and other pups." Sheriff Wright added, "We won't contact the families for another eight to ten hours until we get all the facts and bodies identified first." Paul was amazed at the pretty black woman, wondering why she chose her profession. It was amazing she had won the election. Paul looked at her and smiled, it was uncharacteristic of Paul, but he felt she was under terrific stress and couldn't show her personal and sheer sorrow of people she protected – now dead; Paul attempted to hug her, and quickly learned not to touch the uniform. "Hey," she quickly advised, "I'm sorry, I know you meant well Sir, but I kind of live on the edge when on duty and uniform; they call this crap, "Hypervigilance," I know you meant well."

The woman leaned over and gave Paul a safe-distance hug, and then thanked him for understanding the difficulty of the situation. Paul said he understood, and apologized, but he really had no clue. The squawk of the radio microphone next to her ear advised a rescue boat was headed in with only five bodies, their "ETA in five".

The noise prompted the Sheriff to call a deputy on the radio to hurry with the, (hopefully accurate) list of people that should have been on the ship. A deputy advised there was only seven on the list, (instead of the anticipated eight) that he was expediting to the Sheriff's location. There were a lot of "10-codes" flying over the radio to try and conceal the tragedy, but radio enthusiasts and ham radio operators soon leaked the information. The local radio station, *"KCBY"* would be considerate and cooperate with law enforcement, and they regretfully, had covered these kinds of tragedies before.

Paul had tagged along with Sheriff Wright, knowing with all the law enforcement in the immediate area, nothing would be at risk at the clinic. Following and healing like a good puppy, at a safe distance; Paul arrived at the chosen area to meet the boat, (it sounded like they would be going out for the skipper and first mate in hopes of finding them after unloading the five bodies recovered).

The deputy arrived with the list of names, almost fearing the information he was holding. Like a well-oiled machine, all the pieces to a puzzle were culminating nicely; Paul muttered something about a great job of teamwork by the Sheriff and her Deputies. It was a purposeful muttering that Paul was certain to capture her ear-shot.

"Okay folks use the "Strider" gurneys to transport these pour souls over to the vet's place, he'll show you where to store them, move only one at a time – carefully," the Sheriff barked loudly – with a little bite!

Paul assisted in getting the doors open for the power gurney's journey. The two deputies' radios chirped at the same time, another deputy ready at the Hospital for ambulance cleared traffic, when needed. Both deputies clicked a quick "10-4 at the 10-20" and Paul began staging the bodies on every available treatment table available. They were hauntingly blue and pale, after the sea had spit them out. The deputies were working flawlessly, being respectful for the fallen sailors. Paul had never seen tattoos on a blue, drowned corpse before. It was also hauntingly sad, etching an image into the depths of his soul, forever.

Another tweak of the radios confirmed the County Coroner was in route from Coquille, via another, final deputy. A network of strategically placed red lights would carve up North Bend and Coos Bay, for ambulances to safely move the bodies, and the Morgue had been awakened and manned. Things were going so smoothly, Paul began realizing what this type of preplanning that was required to be enacted and flexed, upon the needs. He appreciated the teamwork and being a part of a plan, that he never knew he was a part.

The five bodies were recovered, the deputies then began taking obligatory photographs to treat it as a crime scene until the investigation was concluded. Paul seemed pretty sure they all drowned at sea, but he supposed someone could have caused the capsizing, (it seemed the culprit was Mother Nature – or some Queen Crab maybe.) One of the deputies started to mutter something about, "the bar took three last year". He quickly took another click of the camera and quit talking when the Sheriff came inside to confer with the Coroner, upon his arrival. Paul knew the deputies were within an ear-shot, so he said loudly, "Sheriff, your team is phenomenal, all this coordination, before you even advise the poor families that will be impacted by this!"

"In this business, telling families their loved one is gone," the Sheriff purposely paused to gain the impact of her deputies, "It's either Wright or Wrong, and we will get it right!"

"Get it Wright the first time!" the entire crew yelled simultaneously. The Sheriff thanked them all for crawling out of bed, leaving their families for hours and assisting, she dismissed a few and asked the others to, "carry-on". They all departed, leaving just Paul and the Sheriff. She then cussed, "shit, I forgot to thank you – in front of them!" She scribbled something in a black, leather, basket-weaved book, "I really will send you an official thank you letter this week, it's really terrific of you helping us stage these bodies in your work area, until moved and placed in the morgue."

"It was great being a temporary part of your team, I'm sorry we had to work together under these circumstances, I honestly feel safe with you at the helm; sorry pun intended," Paul stuttered briefly. He felt like he was maybe flirting with her, since he hugged her earlier. He extended his hand in a professional manner, she shook it, and apologized for leaving but the hope of finding the final two bodies was still there and she wanted to check in and coordinate still.

She left, thinking that this public entity could be a useful resource in the future since they hadn't utilized the office before, but it was uniquely located. She was scribbling in her notebook again, as the five corpses began to sit up behind Paul.

Paul fell to the floor in a wrenching second, it was a stabbing pain, but familiar in the kidney region! He had totally forgotten to think of the "rules for use" of the healing, but it was too late, the quintet behind him, were beginning to flail and yell out loud! The ruckus inside was quickly escalating, Paul was uncovering people that were covered by white sheets, they were hysterical! The attention finally demanded the Sheriff to come back inside, she found Paul trying to silence five survivors of the Peggy Sue – lost at sea with the Captain and her First Mate!

Paul could only scream at the weapon – wielding Sheriff, "It wasn't me!" He thought to effectively pause, and say, "Please, put your weapon away!"

Sheriff Wright wasn't quite sure why she had drawn her weapon, it was just instinct. She holstered her duty weapon, and cried, "What the hell is going on here?"

Paul played as coy as he could with his new-found friend, "I don't know, it just happened!" Paul tried explaining, "I was in the other room, and I was going to call staff to cancel their day schedule to come in, and the next thing I know I heard what you heard. How are you going to explain this?"

Sheriff Wright smiled, "How are you going to explain this? I wasn't with the five, when this happened, but we need to care for them now!" She hit her microphone, but her shaking hand didn't activate it. She spoke at the radio – volume, but no one heard her except Paul, "I need all those ambulances now!" With no response, she realized no squelch had followed, she over-compensated by tearing the microphone off her shoulder, repeating the order even louder. All deputies quickly confirmed the radio – transmitted order. Paul and the Sheriff began helping by performing first aid and calming the victims.

A trail of ambulances began arriving, but they had no overhead lights on and didn't seem to be in a hurry. The Sheriff barked a "Code 3" and lights lit up and they were then rushing to assist! The first responders from the rescue boat, the local Coast Guard vessel, and other emergency response lit up the night. People were flowing in and out, survivors were quickly assessed, and transport quickly followed. Paul was amazed at how quiet it was a short while ago, he felt like he was in downtown Portland now. He was trying to think about how he was going to answer for all this, how to perhaps explain it away. The Sheriff was pointing her fingers at her own eyes, then pointed the same fingers back at Paul; indicating, "I'm watching you!"

Paul asked her quickly if he could go home for now, it was an exciting evening, but the Sheriff said he had to wait, at least until he could lock up. She mentioned something about talking to him about all this. He was desperately tired, he didn't want to answer any questions, he just had some stabbing pain in his kidney region, and he really could just use some rest. He simply faked fainting and fell onto the carpet in the foyer.

The on-site EMT's advised another one needed for the ambulance, and the Sheriff came to his side quickly, trying to rouse the faking victim. "Are you okay Mr. Baldwin?" she kept trying to gain his attention and he kept faking unconsciousness. He thought, maybe a little leg shake may sell the act. But the pressure point that Sheriff Wright applied, brought Paul to an "Ouch!" that followed out loud. The Sheriff patted him lightly and said, "it's okay we'll send you to the hospital too, to get checked out and released" she smiled. Paul knew that she was aware he was playing victim; but she seemed to sense his need to just go and get out of all this. Paul handed the Sheriff the keys, and thanked her again, as the ambulance whined out onto the street.

Paul had never ridden in an ambulance before, it was kind of cool, it was like a limo, but with cool stuff surrounding you…as they plugged him into it. The EMT was asking for his blood type, Paul never really thought about it much, he wasn't sure…it was "O" something. He had given blood once, but didn't remember much about it, except the cookies afterward; when he was young. "I'm perfectly fine now, I assure you," Paul attempted to release himself from further examination, after second thought.

"We'll let the doctors look at you, and then you can go sir," the young professional spouted his usual response. Paul planned to escape as soon as possible, after getting this getaway vehicle stopped. He didn't know what the doctors would find, but he also didn't want to know what they could find. After a doctor seen him, he recommended Paul seeing his personal physician and he ate a sandwich, he called a cab and they took him to his house, leaving the pick-up at the office, and a Sheriff with his keys. He had a hide away key for the house, so he got in quick enough. He took a sleep-aide and decided to face this nightmare in the morning, talking to his bed aloud, "Where have you been…?"

Chapter 11

Cara couldn't have been much help that night, nor did Paul see it necessary to involve her in this nightmare; Paul didn't text her to even mention the affair. She awoke Paul around eight in the morning. It would normally be a great and welcomed visit; but he had about three hours sleep…after running the "oh shit" factor through his head for quite some time that morning instead of sleeping.

Paul didn't answer the doorbell, he dreamed it. Cara shifted into, "I'm concerned, so I'll pound on the door" mode. Paul had his key, and Cara couldn't open the door; the key was missing from its hiding place. Cara shifted into some higher, woman alert, pounding the door with a rock, before calling the 911. Paul opened the door quickly, but the rock stopped about half an inch from his face.

"Where is the key, what were you doing, did you sleep last night, you look terrible, did I wake you?" Cara launched into the questions that Paul wasn't even prepared to drink coffee yet.

"Whoa!" Paul tried to slow the bombardment, "Come in and just let me answer all your questions when I get a cup of coffee or two going!"

"Sounds great!" Cara responded, like nothing was wrong in the world and she was settling down just a bit. "You had me going pretty good there for a while," she laughed, Paul didn't.

He was purposely going to try to answer truthfully, Cara wanted the truth, but Paul wanted to try and cushion what he was about to explain. He didn't want her to worry about him, and it was a bit like spilled milk anyway, he thought.

"When I got home, the Coos County Sheriff called me, they had lost some men on the bar, two haven't been recovered, but I helped by loading them into our clinic, I forgot and touched them all, they all are alive, and the Sheriff returned just to see them awaken and start screaming!" Paul paused, turned, and placed his head on Cara's shoulder and wept, "It's all out there, I don't know if I can hide this one…" He told her he had faked fainting, and that the Sheriff would have his keys, to investigate and tag the area as a possible crime scene or answer to what had happened.

"How many were resurrected," Cara asked, concerned for Paul. Did you feel okay, did you faint, has the doctors checked you out?"

"I told you, I faked the fainting," Paul defended the truth a little, "I'm okay, there were five men total, I'm sure their families freaked out when the deputies told the families about the accidental deaths, and then they pop up alive and all…" He corrected himself, "I don't know if the families were told of the death, or simply advised they had survived the shipwreck."

"We will have to think of a story, or something," Cara began, as the gears in her head were spinning with mock answers. "Wait a minute, you side-lined my question," Cara looked at Paul's crying eyes, "Did you have a Doctor examine you, are **you** okay?"

"I had a bit of a pain, briefly I guess, when I was alone, the Sheriff went outside, so he didn't see, if I did maybe," Paul answered truthfully. "I didn't want to worry you, but yea, I'm okay and the doc checked me out; I didn't want them to look too deep into this thing." Paul minimized his pain a bit, but he knew Cara may be dragged into this thing, and he didn't even know what he feared about what might happen to her.

As Paul was finishing up his "Readers Digest" version of what had happened to Cara, a Sheriff cruiser pulled up and the inevitable Sheriff holding keys approached the door. Paul motioned Cara to his bedroom – reluctantly; he hadn't made the bed yet. Paul headed for the door hoping that Cara wouldn't make any noise, or the Sheriff may not be as sharp or alert.

"Hey, there's my keys and favorite Sheriff," Paul blurted out as he opened the door.

"Yes Sir," she smiled warmly, but cautiously. "Is there anything I should know about before I enter the house?" Sheriff Wright asked. She paused because she observed the second bicycle and it was an open-ended question that allowed a person in the public to just speak out nervously or self-disclose without her really prying.

"Like what, for crying out loud?" Paul wisely answered the question with a question, impressed by her experience in interviewing practices. "Hey, I don't raise marijuana or anything," Paul mis-directed, "but I may have some animal doctor drugs if you like," he smirked nervously.

"It's crazy," Ms. Wright smiled, "I try not to be a cop one hundred percent of the time, but I don't have a warrant, and you appear to be inviting me inside, sometimes I see something maybe you don't want me to see." She paused effectively, "like bestiality or maybe porn?"

"Come inside," Paul rebounded from the insinuation, "No kinky crap here!" he shook his head in disgust, "I'm a law-abiding citizen, and if you ask me about any stupid-ass necrophilia, I'll insist that you get back into your damn car!"

"Clearly, I've given you the wrong impression," the Sheriff began to apologize, "Honestly Paul," using his first name to personalize the apology, "I needed to thank you for the use of your services, your personal building, an indescribable and probably miraculous experience, and to return your keys." She explained her past experiences, which warranted her asking before entering.

Cara was totally impressed with the candidness of this female leader in the county and state. Cara didn't know how many women Sheriff's there were, but she knew it was probably a warranted position that was rare. Besides, she thought, she had voted for her. Impressed with the Sheriff, Cara wondered if she should attempt to crawl out the window silently. She decided not to test the woman in the other room, she would simply be silent and eavesdrop.

Paul seemed to be handling this situation quite well, Cara was impressed with her boss and boyfriend. He didn't sweat any bullets and he seemed to be dodging her questions well. He had made some coffee, so he offered her and cup as she apologized once again, sitting down at the table, she placed the keys next to the napkin holder on the table. Paul thanked her and set down the "peace treaty" coffee. She simply said she liked it black, so he didn't offer her anything, although Paul was glad that Cara couldn't see him as he was gazing into a very beautiful Sheriff.

"I didn't vote for you…but I'm really glad that you were elected," Paul said honestly. The Sheriff took a sip of coffee and answered with another opening, by simply saying, "Uh huh". Paul felt like she was believing him, "I would love to tell you how five sailors get a second chance on life," Paul added, "but I have no answers for you."

Paul hadn't lied, but he didn't answer as to how or what happened. "I see, any help in suggesting an answer to the families of the sailors?" she asked honestly.

"Did you tell the families they were dead, and then have to amend the report and advise their men survived?" Paul asked.

"Absolutely not," the sly woman responded, "I will not have inaccurate information flowing out of my office." She explained how they were going to hold off on the informing of the survivor's families…which allowed her to advise that they saved the men. "But then I suppose I filed a false report…because you really saved them, didn't you?" she grinned a bit as she gazed back into his eye's; making Paul want to tell the whole truth, and nothing but the truth.

"Sheriff, you seem to like facts," Paul spoke as he was thinking what he was going to say, as he continued, "You were there, the bodies were there, when I returned from washing up, the bodies seemed to come alive; and then you came in to assist me," Paul said truthfully, in hopes that it would fly.

"That's not much help," the Sheriff began, "but I suppose that much is true, I just don't think that anyone, (including me) will believe the truth." She explained that she got lucky on her deputies not leaking the death – to life thing; by delaying the bad news delivery, it never shocked the families to know the men had survived, and each man was so happy with renewed life they didn't say anything. She thanked him; but warned him that some people in small towns simply make stuff up and then it rumors for a while. She offered her assistance if anyone became a real noisy or threatening rumor spreader. Paul thanked her, he felt like he had made an ally.

Cara waited in the bedroom even though the Sheriff had left, Paul retrieved her after he sat for a second and took another sip of coffee. Cara came out, asking if she still had the day off as they both had planned before the shipwreck. Paul assured her that she wouldn't be doing anything at work because of the whole CSI stuff, and he felt as though maybe the two of them could spend some time together, and to avoid the world today as much as possible.

His partner, Dick Spencer called and asked about him knowing something about the yellow ribbon that circled the circumference of their office and clinic. Paul gave him a briefing and didn't mention the five men. The local paper, "The World" simply listed two sailors lost at sea; but didn't say too much about the five survivors. Regretfully, the counties along the coastline must list people lost at sea now and then; it came with the territory. All the media and the various Public Information Officers knew their beds were made, when they took the job.

Paul thought the whole thing blew over, but when he and Cara returned to work the next day for business as usual; it was anything but usual. Some investigative reporter from a magazine continued to call and ask to speak to Dr. Baldwin about the wreck of the Greyback; the vessel of the five. Paul advised everyone after the first couple calls asking for him to advise that he was out on house-calls, and the Pet Shelters in the area. Paul found the volunteerism seem to pay a debt, but also besides helping the animals, it helped him escape the clinic and folks in general.

The result was numerous calls to request a call-back to Mr. Grey, in Portland. Paul was born in Portland, but it was unclear why his parents were living there at the time. They were always having to pick-up and move now and then when he was a toddler. He didn't really care for the big city that was truly connected by various bridges. It was a bit too much hustle and bustle for Paul. He remembered when he was in college once, he had taken the wrong turn at an intersection, (in his attempt to beat the oncoming car) which resulted in him driving down the Portland Rose Parade, he waived like a real Rodeo Queen, laughing all the way!

He often wondered how many drivers have gotten confused in the multi-cloverleaf freeway intersections to bridges of no return. To live and drive in Portland, Oregon you almost had to know the Oregon Trail history. Paul didn't get it.

As Paul exited the office a bit early, (after returning from his rounds) the slick SL-500 slithered into the parking lot. The Mercedes seem to be moving – even when sitting still. It was more impressive than the guy that got out and yelled at Paul, "Hey fella, can you direct me to Dr. Baldwin?"

Paul quickly yelled back from his bicycle, "He's going to be back here any minute!" smiling as he lied and peddled off quickly. It appeared he had given the guy the slip, but chances are; he couldn't avoid this character forever. No one was waiting at his house when he locked his bike, grabbed the mail and stepped inside, locking the door. Cara and he had decided to communicate with each other each night on the phone, playing it cool for now. It seemed like a good idea; especially when Cara had this slick suit and tie show up asking to interview her. She declined and advised she had only worked at the Vet Shop for a very short time. She must have sold it, because the guy wandered off; probably to interview Dick Spencer…who will have nothing to say. Paul's interdiction with his previous boss; now partner, liked Paul and his privacy.

Certainly, as predictable as rude, Mr. Grey and his SL 500 were waiting in the parking lot, when Paul drove his pick-up into the lot early. Grey was giving Paul the "once-over" and Paul was giving Grey the "don't bug me" look. The two merged on the sidewalk entrance of the business. Paul had chosen to alternate his bike for the pick-up on purpose.

"Excuse me," the suit and tie began, "I'm the owner of the ship – Greyback."

"Of course, you are, Mr. Grey," Paul said almost ignoring him. "Please step inside to the office, where we can discuss any questions you may have in confidential," he concluded respectfully. A bit surprised the well-dressed man stepped inside and Paul found him a seat, offering to take his coat.

"You are Dr. Paul Baldwin, involved in the rescue of five men here?" he said more than questioned; "Didn't you ride a bike yesterday?" the quick businessman fired a double question.

"Yes, thank you," Paul said ignoring the obvious elephant in the room and any specifics. "You probably would like to see where all this happened," Paul set the stage for the smartass. He continued, "Wasn't it fortunate that the ambulances and EMT's were already here, when the survivors arrived into this building!" Paul lied. He began smiling and tried to make himself look like Peter Falk, he was having fun with it! He would scratch his head now and then, cocking his head to the side, almost squinting with a glass eye, "You know, it was such a busy and dark night to be fighting the wind, as we got the survivors from the Sheriff's boat even before the Coast Guard cutter!" Paul continued his poor imitation of "Columbo" ..."and then just when you thought you had seen everything..." he stalled and paused overtly, "that's when the ole gal at the beach let me know the name of the cute little bastard as it was born!"

"What the," the suit stuttered, "I just have some questions about that night?"

"Sure, sure," Paul continued, "they named it "Jethro!" like on the Clampets!" he laughed out loud, slapping his knee, like an old codger.

"Great, but about the condition of the five dead men," the trickster attempted to lead Paul.

"What, I'm no people doc, but I know the dead don't scream and it was pretty loud!" Paul laughed again. Check that black Sheriff gal, she heard them yell, it's probably in some report; but the birth of a baby Appaloosa, people just ignore that!" Paul half-exclaimed.

"Okay, can we not discuss the birth of the Appaloosa foal that was named Jethro?" Mr. Grey asked as much as pleaded. "I just want to know what you saw when they off-loaded the bodies, here, at this clinic, when you were present?" he tried once more.

"Why didn't you just say so," Paul asked irrelevantly, "two were lost, the Captain, and the First Mate, but those five survivors got lucky that night, and that's that," Paul tilted his head as if all his brains just slid out of the top of his head and out onto the floor!

"Gotcha, thanks Flicka" is all the business man said, as he stood up and went out to his car, driving off and back to Portland, thinking these idiots on the coast..." like so many other Portlanders, as the coast folk wave goodbye, smiling. Paul had dodged another bullet, or at least delayed it.

Chapter 12

Paul felt as though his path may cross, intersect, or just bust the hell out of the idea in meeting Mr. Grey again. He seemed a bit too slick for Paul. Perhaps it was his pride in learning that maybe he wasn't quite the actor he thought; it was much more, Paul could feel Grey's soul would consume his own, Grey was creepy. It was a rainbow, battling a Chinook storm head. Paul only hoped the wind was Eastward like it should be; taking this man back with it.

The rest of the day was spent putting the office, business, clinic, and animals to ease. Paul was happy for most of the day, getting ready to head out just a little early; the phone rang. Paul answered the business phone; the other staff were engaged.

A very nice and cordial woman asked to speak to, "Dr. Baldwin, the Veterinarian please?""

"This is he, how may we help your pet today, Ma'am?" Paul answered back.

"Yea, the Code 3 was called AFTER the bodies were in the pet shop, my friend FLICKA" a familiar man's voice cut in deeply! The line went dead.

The voice gave Paul goosebumps, he shared his good-byes to the staff and headed home on his bike. If he knew what the day had brought, he would have liked to have driven his pickup instead of a bicycle. As he pumped peddles, his brain was cycling through the possible scenario that would or could develop. He found his speed had picked up a bit, like an old quarter-horse familiar with the route; he was pumping fast, close to home speed!

He arrived okay and didn't lock the bike, leaving it prepared for departure-ready. Unlocking the house, feeling a bit silly for being paranoid; Paul quickly scanned the house, but didn't see anything alarming. His cell rang – jolting him a bit like a kid in a scary movie. The ring reminded him of Cara, (she had programmed some special ringtone.)

"Lover, I had that Grey guy waiting at my place," Cara began quietly but excited, "Is this A-whole gonna be a problem for us?"

"No, I hope not," answering truthfully, but nervously, Paul didn't instill the confidence that Cara was looking for at that time. Paul could feel her nibbling on his neck and ear through the phone, "Sweetheart, you are gonna text me a quick email to my home address, about you losing your grandmother, the service will be in Virginia…next week."

"I don't have…okay, let me know when you're being devious, you little stinker!" Cara somehow found some confidence in him. She said she would bike around the waterfront downtown by the restaurants, making sure no one was following; and then meet at Paul's if it was clear. She would lock her bike in his shed.

Paul quickly forwarded an approval for Cara to be gone for at least ten days, forwarding it to Dick to plan for a temp-staff. Normally, it wasn't the way things worked, but Paul was pushing his weight on this one; because he knew he could. He would later tell Dick about him and Cara, it just wouldn't be the time right now. Paul then called Dick's work phone leaving him a message that his health was to be checked out with his Doctor in Eastern Oregon, they would advise him of his tests. Paul knew Dick would take it in the correct context, but for Paul he knew he was about to be tested possibly, and he did have some crazy symptoms that he wasn't going to explain.

Cara arrived finally and secured her bike from sight in the shed, locking Paul's as well. This would probably help to provide access to both young lovers, and perhaps it may confuse onlookers. It seemed like the strangest time to receive a phone call from Pastor Shootee, he apparently had been conducting a service; a member of the congregation had collapsed in the service, she passed peacefully; the religious man apparently laid hands on the lady while she sat on the pew; she regained consciousness and kissed Pastor Shootee's hand! He was loving life and beating death! The holy man was beaming through the phone. Paul congratulated him, (but he had kind of experienced it before.)

The love of God appeared to have apparently spread; although Paul wasn't sure what was happening. He told Cara the tale, she was overwhelmed with emotions. The two needed to disappear for a bit and figure out who this mysterious stranger was, Paul knew a close friend in Reedsport, it was nearby, and they believed it would be a safe house, they would plan from there; but Paul knew he would have to protect Cara. Upon their arrival in Reedsport, Paul was receiving a text on his phone, the subject line was a request to meet with Mr. Grey. Paul would settle into Reedsport, take care of Cara, and then address the issue with Grey.

Paul couldn't figure out why this city slicker wouldn't just file some insurance claim, (if he owned the boat) and then leave the coast and all alone? The lovely smell of honeysuckle mixed with something else familiar, blooming next to the walkway. The beautiful house had quick access to Highway 101, but it was well-situated, and the front lawn was freshly mowed, cut grass was in the air. Inside the house was equally beautiful, it was obvious the owners enjoyed being Oregon Duck fans. Paul found friendship in the couple upon his arrival to the area. They were golfing but had texted for the two on how to find a spare key and get comfortable.

The two found some fresh crab in the refrigerator, nacho chips, and shredded pepper-jack, and a quick microwave minute later, they enjoyed munching on Paul's favorite. A beer was added because the two had just begun to capture their nerves a bit. A loud knock interrupted their snack; there were several reporter-looking people from out of nowhere, lining up and ganging up at the doorway! Paul shushed Cara, although it wasn't necessary, so she slapped at his shoulder instinctively and quietly. She gave him the look, that warned him to back-off!

She then reconsidered, grabbed him forcefully, and tugged him over and to the floor, hugging him quietly and comfortingly. Paul whispered to Cara something about their phones may have been tracked, she shook her head in agreement to replace them. Reluctantly, the two agreed to ditch their phones in the boat that was parked under a carport in the back. Paul couldn't figure out why Journalists would be gathering, maybe the house owner won another golf tournament, or Grey was at work. He planned to send Cara with both phones out back, while he addressed the crowd gathering out front, trying to figure this out as he went along.

"Hey folks," Paul yelled to about a dozen people waiting out front and knocking on the door and ringing the bell, "If you all been told I won the lottery, he's just pulling one of his jokes again!" Paul tried to give the impression that someone was pranking him, laughing and easing the crowd of people.

"Aren't you the Veterinarian, that shot his partner, and then ran off with one of the office gal's?" the inquisitive liar continued, "this looks like you..." he said as he held up a photograph of Paul.

"The cops will be here soon," someone said amongst the crowd. Paul yelled to the crowd, "I was on my way to the Synagogue!" It gained the crowds attention, none appeared to be of Jewish faith, but it gained Cara's attention, she knew where to go by herself. Paul used his hands to hush the distracted crowd, making a bit of a spectacle, he leaped from the porch and front door onto the lawn in front of him.

"I am a vet," Paul began, continuing to distract everyone in front, while Cara escaped out the back, destroying the phones and then pitching into the boat, "I live in Coos Bay, I'll certainly go with the police, but I haven't hurt anyone, someone is pulling a practical joke on all of you!" Paul was hoping that Dick wasn't dead, (again).

A police cruiser from the Reedsport P.D. showed up, asking Paul to come quietly and cooperate, so he turned around, was cuffed and the officer appropriately read him his "Miranda rights". He advised that Paul was under arrest for the murder of his associate. He was being pulled down into the dark depths of some fake news.

Reedsport is at the edge of Douglas County, but Coos Bay was a short drive and then you were in Coos County. Counties often utilized different resources; Coquille was the newer and bigger jail, so it was decided a State Police would escort the City P.D. to the jail in Coquille. Paul continued quietly, knowing Cara would be safe now, he would catch up to her after all this was cleared up.

The Coos County Sheriff Wright was at the jail to meet them as the cruisers arrived with the wanted murderer. She bravely reached out her hand which held a handwritten note, which had written in blood apparently, "Paul Baldwin..." She thought she was holding a note that a murdered man had scribbled his to point to his killer. Paul quickly tried to establish rapport with Sheriff Wright, "You know Dick and I, and you know I could never kill Dick, I've been with Cara, where was Dick's body found anyway?"

"Great," the clever Sheriff began, "Tell us where we can find her to substantiate this." Paul wasn't about to tell where she was. "Help me – to help you," the Sheriff began with her trained interview technique. "This will go a lot easier if you just cooperate, Paul" she continued to personalize the interview. Paul shook his head negatively, not believing what was going on. "Process him," the Sheriff ordered reluctantly, "It's a strip search, and of anything on you or your clothing, to prevent suicide, but you're not going to hurt yourself, are you?" she explained.

"No," Paul shook his head, "but I hope you do your usual thorough job, to free me as soon as possible." Paul knew she would get to the bottom of this, but he didn't want to involve Cara, and he certainly knew that Dick was probably writing a warning to Paul, that had to be why he scribbled it.

One of the Sheriff deputies, entered the building holding a CD, advising the Sheriff that he pulled some video from the bank exterior cameras, it captured the corner of Dick's house. The deputy simply stated that a vehicle fitting the description of a stolen vehicle had pulled up next to Dick's house at the estimated time of death. He also added that an ODOT camera on the Highway 101 construction site to Reedsport had Paul's vehicle around the same time.

Sheriff Wright quickly interceded the arrest by reaching across and uncuffing the previous murder suspect, apologizing; she admitted there were two hotline tips indicating Paul was the murderer, at the address where they found Dick and the note. "I'm sorry Paul," she began, we seem to have not gotten this one right," she smiled warmly.

"You and your deputies got it right," Paul surprised her with a smile, "I'm just glad you all put this puzzle together, before the strip-search thing!" He asked if someone could please take him back to his vehicle in Reedsport, a radio squawk later and the impounding of his vehicle was stopped and ordered to be delivered to the Veterinary Clinic for Paul to pick it up.

"I'd like to say it's been a pleasure, but I will be assisting you all in the death of my partner," Paul said excusing himself quickly, "You can expect my full cooperation, I want this murderer found!" Paul asked Sheriff Wright to personally drive him to the clinic to pick up his car, pushing the boundaries a bit, because he knew he could.

"Certainly," the beautiful black woman said, "we appreciate your assistance." She had turned on a dime, Paul appreciated the chance to figure out this whole thing. He was being framed and quite well; maybe the Sheriff could share some facts, and not believe this fake news she was fed. "Right this way Paul," she led him out of the hornet's nest, unlocking the doors to her undercover cruiser, with concealed emergency lights. The two whizzed out of Coquille, (with no fear of receiving a ticket for speeding) and Cara was safely heading in the opposite direction; almost to I-5 freeway, headed for Paul's parent's in Eastern Oregon.

"So, who is at the top of your list of people that want to frame you for a murder of a friend and coworker?" Sheriff Wright asked as she was driving.

"I have to think it's this stranger that has been around asking questions," Paul began, "I think maybe he was the owner of the boat that cap-sized."

"The guy drives a pretty Mercedes," the Sheriff chirped in, "The Greyback" was owned by a fellow in Alaska, I'm working with the insurance company now. She took her eyes off the highway briefly to look at Paul, "The Mercedes is a super doctor, assigned to a big pharmaceutical company that may be connected to the government," Sheriff Wright seemed to be warning Paul, "every time I get close to his credentials, I get a call from the government advising me to cease and desist."

As the vehicle arrived at its destination, Sheriff Wright took Paul's hand to ensure his attention, "You're a nice guy, and the kindness to animals – reflects you have a big heart, but I'm afraid you're way over your head on this one, you should take a vacation or something and I'd watch over your back, if I were you."

Paul shook his head in affirmation, but inside he knew a bit more to the story that he couldn't divulge to the Sheriff quite yet; besides she wouldn't ever believe him. He would have to apparently be careful and try to blend into the subterfuges that may come at him; or be prepared to roll with the punches.

Paul had more questions than answers, and his father didn't teach him to back down from a bully; he would have to start down a path he wasn't fond of taking; but he knew that Cara was safe now and he would not be afraid to get his hands dirty. He drove back home, trying to put the pieces together in his head.

He thought that he would start first thing in the morning, planning on his routine, work, contacting Cara, and looking into Dr. Grey. He was certain that he may get to the bottom of this whole thing, avoiding discussing any ability that he may have, or involving Cara. After he entered the house and found two goons and Dr. Grey sitting on his sofa – it was apparent the conversation wasn't going to wait. Nothing puts a person on defensive; than entering your home and finding someone there that wasn't invited.

Chapter 13

Paul reached for his cell phone to call the authorities and a tall man, pulled back a trench coat to reveal a box that had a blue light. The cell phone couldn't get any coverage for its first time. It was looking as desperate as Paul.

"I suppose, I might as well put this away," Paul tried hard to smile, surmising the situation, he believed the device rendered his phone useless. For the moment, Paul knew that it would be a useless attempt to do anything about the intruders. Dr. Grey or whomever he was calling himself, was in charge of the moment.

"You're a difficult veterinarian to arrange an appointment with," Dr. Grey smirked, "I'm afraid the situation was dire enough for me to come to you!"

"You probably don't own a pet," Paul guessed with certainty, "although you certainly surround yourself with critters!" Paul punched back.

"I suppose, if I did have a pet, it would be a woman," the pompous and wealthy man interjected, "at least then she would perform a function." The disregard for pets, and now women, made Paul a bit angrier than he was before. Dr. Grey seemed to be a cold-hearted bastard from Paul's aspect. "You would do well, not to angry these critters, I hire them for a purpose, and they are good at most," Dr. Grey warned.

Paul cautiously moved toward the kitchen in hopes of finding something to aid him in the situation, if needed. "If you ever need someone to euthanize them," Paul paused his slow creeping to make a point that certainly rhetorical.

"You certainly like to take chances," Dr. Grey smiled spinelessly, "I've warned you about these men, don't test them by some silly heroic action that would most certainly kill you!" The creepy man patted the sofa he was sitting in, "Please, just sit down and discuss this matter, and then I promise my men and I will leave you in peace."

"I'll hold you to that," Paul said, as he slid down across from the possible threat. "The sooner we get this done, the sooner you can leave my house!" Paul stated firmly. "You seemed determined to make up your own story," Paul suggested as he got a closer look at the runt.

"As a doctor, I'm concerned about the possible side effects of the Bird Fire epidemic, I work for the World Healthcare Interagency Program, or W.H.I.P. for short." Dr. Grey explained. He shrugged his scrawny shoulders, in an effort to excuse the acronym. "We're doing some excellent work, and we share our information around the world!" Dr. Grey leaned forward toward Paul, "None of my colleagues have found any valuable information," he shook his head, "except news in small ripples about you, keep surfacing."

"You mean rumors, conjecture, poor media, and sea stories around here?" Paul played naïve, "I hope you're not breaking into everyone's houses over this!"

"On the contrary," Dr. Grey leaned back into the sofa, "people that are reunited with their family, after dying at sea!" The runt stood quickly, "Do not test me, and don't take me for a fool, I know you're hiding something, and if you want to be provided unlimited funding and assistance, you'll contact me – before I have to contact you again!" Dr. Grey dropped a calling card on the end table. He motioned for the men to exit, and the orchestrated mess that resulted in them raking things off shelves on their way to the door. One goon opened it, and then they sandwiched Grey into the middle as they filed out the front door; an engine nearby revved and they were gone.

Paul picked up the items fallen or broken on the floor, wondering if it would do any good to call law enforcement at all. The "WHIP" card had all kinds of numbers on it; from fax to Hong Kong. Paul put it aside for future review, but he wasn't impressed with how the organization interacted with potential future members.

Paul felt as though an organization that is motivated to wipe out disease…should be a worthy cause, instead of a conglomerate bent on scare tactics; or hired muscle. Paul fell back on the rules that he had worked up with Cara, and evil or bad was number two, since the number three on the list was how Paul felt about it…the obvious decision was to not trust this outfit or assist them with his ability.

Paul run the list through his head again, in order; never for money, not for bad or evil, how Paul felt about the issue, and lastly…never animals. The list seemed to serve him well. Cara and he believed that this could guide them in the use of The Healing. WHIP was well funded, government backed, (and apparently used Dr. Grey as a strong political influence, and researcher.) Paul also now knew they had a device to jam a cell phone at the ready, providing him knowledge in the future, if they were to meet again.

After the runt and his idiots had broken into his house, Paul didn't trust the internet, the rooms, or even his phone. It was obvious that these people wouldn't be above bugging his place, (if they were going to break in.) Paul exited and quickly went to his next-door neighbor, she was a kindly widow that he did accomplished tasks that she would find from time to time. He asked her if he could use her internet, (although he knew she would say agree to it, since Paul installed it for her the previous year.)

He sent Cara a quick email that he knew she would find on her private user-name profile. She would be worried about him, but now she would know not to trust Paul's house. As Paul sent it, he knew that anything put down into an email is potentially compromised, depending on the operator and the system. Paul advised her to purchase another smart phone and to encrypt it; he would do the same and then somehow, they would re-connect via his family. This could help protect her; Paul would do whatever was necessary to try and keep her safe. This would free him to do whatever he might have to do – without worrying as much. Dr. Grey and WHIP could not be underestimated; Paul kept being uncomfortably surprised by them.

Cara would not stand by patiently, she had to know more about this information Paul was sharing; she researched WHIP and found some information to share with Paul the next time they communicated. Apparently, the international organization was primarily aimed at targeting world health issues, (like famine, potable water, irrigation, etc.). But for some reason, they were shifting their focus to Bird Fire epidemic now. Accelerating time tables, scrounging money from resources; even throwing around some grants for people that assisted in their cause. This almost didn't make much sense to Cara since she and everyone else had recovered from the temporary ailments. The rest of the world had moved on or appeared to have fought off the illness and effects months ago. It was no longer a threat, as far as anyone knew the treatments and time seem to dissipate.

Cara thought that perhaps some people had side-effects which may require an international health agency would want to assist and help cure any stricken by the ailments. Her imagination got the best of her a little, Cara wondered if maybe this guy working for WHIP went rogue, or maybe some government agency thought about weaponizing the idea…there were all kinds of possibilities. Cara had some addresses, contacts, and information about the organization that she thought it would help Paul when they communicated again.

Paul had personally contacted work and made an excuse for he and Cara being absent for an extended time, Dick Spencer didn't like having to cover the clinic by himself, but he owed Paul more than he could ever thank him. He curiously asked Paul if perhaps Cara and he were eloping, or at least romantically involved. Paul must have grinned or smiled at the wrong time, because Dick said, "Say no more". It was nice being a partner, but it was even nicer being a hero that brought your partner back to life! It was a golden parachute that Paul had only to pull the ripcord.

After some quick pre-trip gathering of items, packing some essentials, and taking out some cash from the bank for expenses; Paul locked his credit cards up and went to concealment with cash. Next, he went around town to the usual places and advised how he was going on a vacation to a theme park in California. He figured if anyone came around asking, they would get a happy face from a local and a lie about a theme park destination. Paul had laid out a very good basic plan to disappear; the game was afoot.

Leaving his vehicle, storing his bicycle at a friend's; Paul headed out and quickly got a ride hitchhiking – to Portland. He headed into the Rose City to meld in, disappear, and figure out what his next move was going to be. The worries of Cara, the shop, partner, house, and everything else drifted away as he settled into a fleabag hotel that wasn't going to notice anything – ever! Paying day to day in cash would help keep him invisible, he had packed his work clothes he had previously purchased from the local Hospice store, so he could pull off the street-living, drab, and invisible look.

He would let his beard grow, simply to change his appearance, but he wouldn't have to worry about shaving for a while. He knew the bridges, overpasses, and places where homeless would hang out for some little bit of shelter. He kept his MP3 player, since all the loaded songs could be the only comfort he would have available. With a new expendable phone, and his old one locked up and stored, he didn't carry anything that could be tracked. Paul kind of enjoyed the non-responsible behavior for a break, but he knew he couldn't do this for more than a month at most. That would give him time to coordinate and plan some type of anti-WHIP campaign, or at least anti-Grey. It would be a lot easier without all the connectivity that Paul had in Coos Bay. Portland can swallow you up, if you let it.

After the first week of blending in, and accidentally giving food to a homeless black man, Paul quickly became friends with the earthly, lack of possession-people; earning the name, "St. Paul". It seemed like an honorary title, so Paul didn't object. In reflection, he later thought it would have been a good idea if he wouldn't have absorbed the name. Paul soon learned the names of some of the characters that were just verily living, on the street. He found it easiest to disappear among those that have been forgotten. Society had turned it's back on these, some had addiction problems, others had legal, some had both. What the weather didn't kill, the police didn't arrest, or weren't committed – the few were becoming, the many. Homeless shelters were packed and were most likely a school of crime. Health care is most often absent and non-existent; but when diabetics don't take insulin, and HIV needle sharers believe that since they're positive already – what can hurt them further? These lost souls were the castaways, the discarded, societies shunned and unassisted.

It was here that Paul met a prostitute named, "S-Phyliss" she had suffered from various STD's over the years, but the syphilis had taken her sight in one eye, (that was cloudy now) and her mental capacity was growing less stable, (probably weekly). She was certainly guilty of stealing fruit or snacks that were readily available from the sidewalk. Some vendors considered it an acceptable loss and attributed it to the mad lady. She was probably also guilty of the foulest cussing that anyone had ever heard! Most people avoided her, simply because they didn't want to start an argument and suffer the slings and arrows that her tongue could wield in words. She often had a handful of sexual clients that wanted unspeakable things in unimaginable ways.

She bumped into Paul, while running from a vendor that was stupidly chasing her, or the green apple that she was carrying. She threw out some verbal abuse that involved terrible swear words that ended with, "a coconut up your butt!" Paul laughed at the incident and comedy of it, but it made the prostitute angry, because she naturally thought he was laughing at her. It is a terrible thing to have an angry prostitute yield a switchblade knife, when she thinks you are taunting her! Paul thought quickly of the rules to using The Healing; he actually felt sorry for her, but there was no reason not to help her. He thought she wasn't bad, she needed – good.

"I'm so sorry," Paul began, "my mistake, please forgive me." He smiled as warmly as possible, trying not to stare into the eye of the witch. Paul genuinely believed that this woman needed a second chance in life, he would find a way to touch her and focus to see if he could still use the almost forgotten gift.

As Paul reached out to shake her hand, but the witch turned quickly away and fled the still angry vendor. Paul slowly followed her, finding her eating the apple in the shadows of a nearby building. She jolted as Paul came into her view. She then put the past few minutes together, and recognized Paul from the earlier encounter. She reached into her pocket and wielded the knife, without the blade extended – as a warning.

"Hey, I'm not here to hurt you," Paul said disarmingly, "I'm a paying customer girl, here…you demand payment up front for a BJ, right" as he handed her a couple twenty-dollar bills. She quickly grabbed the money and yanked it out of his hand, putting it down her front into a vault that would remain untouched.

"Well, get it out!" Phillis demanded sternly. "I ain't got all day," she laughed as she swallowed another piece of apple.

Paul said quickly, "Hey, just let me see inside your mouth" as he reached toward the woman's mouth. As expected and anticipated, she grabbed his hand to tell him not to touch her; which resulted in her holding Paul's hand long enough for him to work his magic.

Instantly Phyliss fell to her knees, sobbing, she snuck out only a few words, repeating over and over, "I can see, I can see, I can see!" Her anger left her body, as her mind wrenched back into gear. Her face gained a renewed glow, her cheeks were now pink, and her teeth were white, Paul thought he saw her breasts move upward in a firm motion, leaving the bra-less woman looking thirty years younger. Her hair was still dirty, her mouth still smelled, but she was a different woman. She smiled a bright and happy smile upward at Paul, but she was still sobbing, "God Bless you, I don't know how you did it, but I'm healed, I feel renewed, thank you, thank you so very much!

Paul simply said, "You have no venereal diseases, let no man infect you again." "You walk healthy out of these shadows; know that you have been given a second chance, cherish it!" Paul smiled rejoicingly and walked away. The once terminal prostitute sat crumpled in the shadows sobbing joyously. She whimpered out a thank you, but Paul was already gone. Paul returned to the terrible room he was staying in and laid down. He hadn't noticed at first, that there was no pain, no after-effect from using The Healing. Finally, it hit him like a brick; no pain! This was reassuring, since now he may not fear harming himself in using the gift. He wondered what changed, why was there a change? He then considered his past use, the dead were brought back to life…but Phyliss wasn't dead, she was ill. He thought that maybe the severity of the use could impact the side-effects. Maybe he could do better out there?

Chapter 14

Paul was still cautious; he was wary of reporters or the media, he was careful in the use of The Healing, and to assess any collaborated harm to himself after the use. He also abided by the rules that he had created in using his gift. While hidden deep in the true hearts of Portland, WHIP would find it hard to track him. He purposely had not contacted Cara for a while, they were both cautious, in case of monitoring by the organization or it's string-puller, Grey.

Dr. Grey stepped into an impromptu meeting of WHIP; he noticed there were a whole lot more people in the meeting room; the meeting population had quadrupled, Dr. Grey grabbed a seat, since people were filing into the back and sides of the large conference room. Dr. Grey had not intended on giving a speech, nor was he comfortable asking pesky questions that have no relevance. His patience was about spent on the efforts toward the coastal veterinarian recently.

There was a loud gavel banging that demanded attention as the panel at the front of the room dictated silence and the beginning of what appeared to be more than the usual meeting.

"If you all will please present your access badges to the security staff that will be deploying through our group, they are simply scanning to verify your clearance for the confidential discussions that will follow," the gavel carrier barked loudly! About a dozen men in black carrying portable scanners, combed the crowd quickly.

One innocent looking woman was quickly surrounded when her apparent forged identification resulted in a negative scan by the security staff. She tried laughing it off, then tried to name-drop, and then she was placed in zip-tie restraints and removed. The scanning continued without anyone else making much of a fuss. Once the men in black had completed their task, their leader pushed a concealed button that resulted in the acoustic tiles along the walls slowly dropping small portable seats that no one in the room anticipated. The security team left as quickly as they arrived; and closed the meeting room door as they left. People took the now available seats and the room quieted even more, quickly.

"This meeting will be the first of many," the gavel was speaking again, "you chosen few will carry the message of this meeting as a burden!" The room now was paying complete attention to the speaker, "You will determine who, will have the need to know, to discuss among your leaders and scientific community." The man took a deep breath, "Quite simply, the Bird-Fire epidemic has dealt us a more problematic after-effect; we are receiving reports all over the world that men have become sterile, at an alarming rate!" If this "Post-Epidemic" continues, our human population may become an endangered species!"

The room instantly roared with conversation, and what was a quiet conference, was now a mass of verbal tirades. The banging gavel was silent, although striking a surface to make an intended noise; it couldn't be heard – nor gain order. The chaos that followed for approximately ten minutes was finally silenced by a large man sitting at the panel, throwing his chair into the table, the pieces flying into a noisy crowd. It seemed to do the trick, because the entire room then gave the very large man silence, and attention. The gavel then could be heard, demanding order once again for controlled conversation to follow. The group didn't figure on this puppy when they began breakfast that morning! This was a game-changer! Children that were a burden; suddenly became the "Love of my Life!"

Everyone had the same questions, "How fast is it spreading, is it contagious, what's being done about it, and lastly; will we have a cure in time?" The nations of the world would have to put aside their bickering, wars, conflicts, and focus primarily on fertility and information sharing. If there was to be hope, the world would find it in their intelligence, and not their weapons. The news, if not carefully safeguarded; and shared cautiously, could result in world business and stock market crashes! Rioting, hospital looting, and even kidnapping could all be results if the group were to leak this information

Dr. Grey was absorbing the information, like everyone else in the room; but he chose not to share any of the "Veterinarian healing on the Oregon Coast" information with the others. He intended on investigating it further, now with renewed vigor, and then they would all come to him; when he saved the day. He imagined he would probably receive the Nobel Peace Prize, not to mention all the money that could be involved in this! Grey decided he would simply be that...neither black or white, but he was too clever to share valuable information of this caliber with a room full of windbags! They would want to ask questions he wasn't prepared to answer; besides the Bird Fire was a separate issue, Dr. Grey had decided.

The henchmen that worked for Dr. Grey hadn't located Paul; with nothing to report, they were combing the coast. A small detail of four men were dispatched to Eastern Oregon to try and verify Paul hadn't contacted family. They were sent on an errand that would fail, since the safeguards were in place. Cara was enjoying Paul's family, safe and sound; no one would be talking; and the small town of Seneca could be very good at protecting its own.

Paul walked into the children's hospital with only fifteen minutes before visiting would be concluded. Paul knew every child here would pass his rules for using The Healing. He had bathed and cleaned his second-hand clothing, so as to present an acceptable appearance as we strolled through the doors. He put on a sad looking face as he tried hard to look devastated, he approached the information kiosk, "I need directions to the floor that has the burn victims, please...I've just flown in!" The frantic request resulted in instant directions to the elevator and floor, with the warning that visiting would be concluding.

Paul exited the elevator, finding the nurse's station to the right, he went left quickly, unaware if he was observed or not. There were a dozen rooms down the hallway, they each had specific equipment for the patient assigned, so there was only one child to a room, (with lots of equipment). Paul looked into the first room, there were no visitors and it was hard to tell if the child was male or female, no hair was left on the burnt scalp.

There was a purposeful effort to enhance the smell, but it made Paul think of burnt hair and pine cleaner mixed in the air with little hope. He looked at a chart that was at the end of the bed, finding a name, "Malcolm" he didn't even awaken the poor, suffering child. He grabbed Malcom's leg and began to rub it slowly, and the multi-colored, and blistered face began to melt away, resulting in a beautiful black boy, awakening from a terrible dream, he looked up with a smile. No hair had returned, but his facial figure and tone were returning. Paul exhaled loudly, and then pulled himself from the healing child.

He went to the next room and found Amy, she was almost without a leg to massage or rub, but by the time Paul had spent a few minutes, her new pink toes, were glistening! She began to cry and then began praying in some language Paul was unknowing, but joy emanated from her! Paul left the room as she was becoming louder, and he ventured into the next room down the hall. His next burn victim was Charles, he had also lost his vision, so his eyes were bandaged. He had no idea anyone was in the room when Paul snuck in.

Paul whispered into Charles ear, he quoted First Corinthians verse on love, he then found only an arm that was not impacted by fire. Paul began rubbing it and purposefully laughing out loud; Charles was a bit frightened at first, but then when his other arm was healed, he used it to peel the white bandages off his eyes as he yelled with glee, "I CAN SEE!!!"

The ruckus Paul had created, caused more than quite a stir; he found it necessary to use the stairs and quickly exit the floor to avoid any confrontations with nurses. He found he was able to use a service elevator to get to the ground floor loading dock access, where he left the building. He would have loved to have stuck around to see the wonderful impact on the three newly healed children; but he was feeling a bit weak. It wasn't too bad, and he made it back to his crappy room without incident. He fell asleep, thinking of the joy he brought to the children in a burn center.

The media and doctors were faced with a conundrum; they could make up reasons for some homeless people claiming to be given a new healthy chance on life, but how do you re-form skin tissue on burn victims – they weren't sure how to even explain the angelic intruder gaining access to a children's burn unit. Regretfully, it brought national media interest; not only Oregon media, but talk-show hosts, mystics, and probably even alchemists!

The media scheduled a circus that took up their good morning, news edition; to display the three children that had been previous burn victims. The appearances would grant future finance to help the children, allegedly. It was a bit of a sideshow; and of course, focused on the result; not the provider of the miracles. Paul didn't mind, since he saw the show from a store television for sale and was trying to enjoy anonymity as well as helping people that needed it the most. Each of the three children tried to emphasize and describe the saintly figure in white that had appeared and healed them, (their descriptions varied, which made Paul laugh).

The Electronics Department kid asked Paul to move on, so he was rudely interrupted from the interesting coverage. Paul headed out and back to his cruddy room, planning his next location to sneak in a "Healing Bomb" and then disappear again. He was careful to alter his route back to the room; he would take an alley now and then. On this one particular occasion, he was jetting through an alley, when he came head-on into some skirmish between some cops and a couple of wanna-be gang members.

There was an exchange of gunfire, Paul could have seen more if he wouldn't have been taking cover behind a large garbage dumpster, (made of steel.) Within seconds, the entire TV episode was unraveled in front of Paul; the result was a dead man, and an injured accomplice being rushed upon by three different response cruisers and their staff. Ambulances could be heard in the background, but the cops were already taping off the area, taking photographs, using chalk to identify the bodies location and proximity to the weapons that were removed; only small tags remained where weapons once laid. The small tag forest included brass casings scattered about randomly; while their bullets were sent to intended specific targets seconds earlier. A couple ambulances were screaming to a halt, police blue and red lights flickered an orchestra of the scene; pulsing with power.

Expended gunpowder and diesel filled the air, with a misty veil of rainy fog; the scene was definitely from some movie; Paul watched intently, trying to keep his distance and find an opportunity to exit "Stage Left" as soon as he could do so without being seen, and subsequently linked to something he wanted no part of.

The cop's attention seemed to be directed toward a vehicle and passenger that demanded it; the Crime Scene Unit and Supervising Medical Examiner were going to be quickly bombarded by the cops to ensure their story was the one heard first. Paul made his way to the alcove that was still a shadow, it was near the dead body of the gangster; but Paul knew it was the only avenue of escape safely. As he slowly and cautiously crept along the concrete, he peered briefly at the body; inside the pocket, (of what used to be a white sport jacket) was the pearl handle of a small pistol.

The handgun was smeared with some blood-stained fingerprints, but it was concealed in a specially tailored pocket of the jacket. Paul thought it might be important to the cops since they must have missed it initially. Paul reached over slowly, watching the background of cops – more than the foreground of the body and weapon. He then simply grabbed the trigger guard of the small handgun with his little finger; and gave it a flick. It was a perfect flick, resulting in easily seeing the weapon. Paul lost his balance just a little, resulting in him breaking his fall by grabbing the ankle of the dead gangster. Paul had no chance to use his rules for The Healing.

The small white cloth that covered the face of the gangster came alive rather quickly! A large bellowing breath; blew the bloody white cloth into the air! The gangly youth sat up just as quickly, resulting in several gold chains clinking noisily. It took Paul by surprise since it was an accidental use of his gift. Paul instantly felt a wave of painful dread through his chest and heart! It was quite strong and all he could do is crawl away slowly from the entire mess. The youth must have looked at his bloody-white sport jacket, the scattered and flagged shell casing forest; and lastly, he must have remembered what had happened minutes earlier.

Paul was almost underneath a park bench about half a block away, when one of the Police saw the previously dead victim sitting up, with a white pearled handgun beside him. The highly trained instinct kicked in, and the young Officer yelled, "GUN!" Instantly the now self-realization of the gangster and his situation kicked in as well. He must have realized from the blood-stained chest area; that he should be dead…and he was about to be dead again! He kicked the small firearm towards the Police, and then began weeping uncontrollably. As the Officer closest approached cautiously, (keeping a bead on his front sight and the perp) he crept close enough to kick the small firearm behind him to the eight or nine Officer's, (that were all sighting the shot to the center mass of the gangster).

The misguided youth that was granted a second chance began apologizing to the Officer that was approaching, "I'm so sorry, I ain't no threat, please forgive me!" The Officer did not let his defensive tactics instructor down, he kept his guard up; reaching for his handcuffs with one hand, he kept a bead on the threat at the same time. The young Officer's tunnel vision was now allowing for the peripheral vision to open up, he could sense the staff behind him with weapons. He holstered and locked his weapon, he then began giving verbal judo directions to the perpetrator. He ensured his body-cam was operational as he began reciting the rights of the individual he was arresting. Everything was by the book.

The still-apologizing, gangster was smiling warmly, placing his hands behind his head, clenching fingers as instructed. The Officer rolled him on his stomach, placing the restraints on and locking the pin, (so as not to continue to become tighter and restrain blood-flow.) The "should-be dead man" got to his feet quicker than the Officer, still smiling, he unleashed a flow of compliments to the Officer, "YOU, are the kind of guy that his mother is proud of; I wanted to be a Police Officer, I'm cool walkin' with you, just tell me what you want, and I'll do it!" God sent an angel to give me a second chance," the man continued, "my life is turning around, thank you God!"

As the two neared the group of Officers, weapons were holstered, and the compliments continued; "You Officers got to know I'm sorry about all this, and it won't happen again," the newly reborn man continued, "God bless you folks, thank you for keeping our city safe!" If there would have been a count of Officer's rolling their eyes in disbelief – the number would have been staggering! Still with the Officer's body-cam running, the arrested man stopped cold in his tracks, seeing Paul move out from the bench cover; under a street light as he exited. "THAT," the man yelled loudly, "Is the angel, that brought me back to life! Thank-You, God bless you!"

Paul heard the thank you, but wasn't sure he did the right thing, since there was no time for using his rules as a standard. He was still hurting, so he took the quickest route back to the dank room, (there was no time for alternate routes!)

Upon returning to the room, he ate some of the stored food and water that he had for an emergency, and then rested the rest of the day. He wondered why this one use of The Healing had caused him so much pain? It could have been a number of reasons, he tried thinking each one through. Maybe it was because it was accidental, or that it was someone that had ill-intentions, or criminal background; perhaps it was just the straw that broke the proverbial camel's back?

Paul finally took a handful of over-the-counter pain killers to knock out his head, (that he seemed to be swimming in, at the time.) As he released his nightly prayers to God, he prayed for the soul of the man that was re-born that evening.

Chapter 15

The plus to having no television, was the silence enough for Paul to get some well needed sleep. It probably was more an over-the-counter unconsciousness – more than sound sleep; but Paul was exhausted and ten hours later he began to get up and around. He ate the last stashed energy bar in the small room for breakfast, but it only made him hungrier. He decided it was about time to try and contact Cara, via the family in Eastern Oregon. Checking the outside of the building, looking around and loitering; it appeared Paul was clear for take-off. He whipped around the corner of the crappy hotel that had his cruddy room, into a nearby alley, no one tailing, no suit watching over a newspaper.

Paul gathered around some group of homeless, under an overpass, they usually had the newspapers, (it helps to start a fire in a can for warmth.) One of the papers had a headline from the coastal region. The author of the article was impressed with the irony that the five sailors that had been saved from a previous wreck of the ship "Greyback" had somehow, aided and assisted to save several men off a crabbing ship that was on fire in the harbor. The article was tipped toward the saved – saving others now, in return. Paul connected the dots of his past briefly.

The buzz among the group was the "burn-angel" that had appeared, healed three kids, and then left on the wings of a giant eagle! Paul smirked a bit when he heard that, he wanted to ride off on the wings of an eagle, it made a great story. No word on Phyliss, Paul was hoping she didn't fall backward into regret again. As Paul worked his way toward the more casual and respectable Portland streets, he began to pick up a sense that WHIP and Dr. Grey were closing in. One electronics store that always had the news on their TV facing the window, gathered flocks of potential customers, and the news fans. Paul dodged quickly, in seeing Dr. Grey being interviewed on the television! It wasn't totally unique for some homeless person to dodge, move, parry, or anything else, as long as you repeat the act, (and then move on) you can pull off normal – homeless pretty easy.

Paul grabbed an expendable cell phone, unwrapped it, and headed back to the privacy of his cruddy room. Paul called his uncle and set up a time when Cara would call him back. Paul also had purchased some energy bars to refill his stash of emergency food for the room. He hoped the mice or rats didn't get into them, but he hadn't seen any yet. Cara called and the two traded real-life adventure stories; Cara told Paul if it was a contest – he won. She asked the cold question that Paul feared, "Tell me about any after-effects from using The Healing?"

Paul didn't want to answer, but he didn't want to lie to her either. He amazed her with the feeling of joy, (instead of pain) when the burn victims were healed; but then he told her about the accidental gangster interaction too. She began crying, worrying for Paul, she made him promise to lay low and not engage anything – or anyone for a while. Paul agreed, he knew she was right, but he didn't tell her about Dr. Grey being in Portland, it didn't come up and he knew it would only worry her more. Paul justified the omission, but he knew it was like telling a lie, and wrong not to tell her.

Just as he was in a somewhat, comfortable sleeping position on the cruddy bed mattress; he thought he was hearing someone in the hall, whispers that were nodding him to sleep. The door cracked as the pressure of the barricade-buster crashed through it; spilling into the tiny room about seven or eight men in black and brandishing guns! They splintered the door and crashed into Paul on the bed, flipping him and restraining him very quickly. Not one word was muttered, hand signals seemed to be the guiding direction, by a single supervisor that was motioning like a tactical mime. They picked him up in a four-man carry; whisking him out of the room and into the corridor, (bumping his head on a wall.)

He had a piece of duct tape placed over his mouth, (that his tongue was wrestling with, making a taste of fiber-plastic and petroleum.) Someone had placed some damn type of mask over his head, so he couldn't be recognized. The entire operation went suspiciously smooth. He was thrown into a vehicle, crammed and injected with a knockout sedative. Paul tried to fight through the sedative – he found himself tumbling down the rabbit hole; feeling only bumps in the road. He thought about trying to listen for sounds, they crossed some railroad tracks…or a bridge…or maybe…he drifted into unconsciousness.

There was a lot of white. White walls, white ceiling, white noise even. It was a constant and soothing type of whirring. Paul kept thinking about waking up, but he was so comfortable; it was a bit of a foggy notion;

but he wanted to do something – anything! He finally felt on the verge of waking, he cracked his eyes open to see the blur of white. It was a man, a doctor, or someone in a white lab coat. He was reviewing a chart, looking at something behind Paul. The odor emanating from the lab coat was at best; sterile, clean, crisp, and an absence of people odor.

"Ah," the lab coat began to realize Paul was awake, "How are we feeling?" Paul found his throat was extremely sore, it hurt to try and talk; it felt as though someone had stuck a cactus down it. Paul definitely couldn't speak, it would be pretty easy for someone to pick up on it. The man smiled, then as his face began clearing, Paul began to drift off once again, with only the words, "We'll take care of you my friend, Flicka".

Paul's head kept asking himself, "Where have I heard that name?" It seemed like his face was itchy, Paul awoke a couple times scratching his face. Sometimes he couldn't move his arm up to scratch his face. At some point, Paul yelled out from the darkness, "KNOCK IT OFF!"

Peeking through the cloud, once again; Paul was squinting and starting to see all the white again. He was having trouble moving most of his body, it was rusty. Slowly, he would try to move his arms, one at a time. There wasn't the familiar strap, no Velcro sound followed. He could move his arm a little, but he was able to move his fingers one at a time. He decided to squint a lot, move very little, and then hopefully learn more about how to stop himself from nodding off into oblivion again.

Trying to look asleep, he would try to gain an idea where he was, and most importantly; how to escape! There was an I.V. drip that was connected to his left arm, he scratched his new beard quickly, then let his hand land onto the liquid line of unconsciousness. He found he could pull the plastic from an insert; and let the fluid drip onto the sheets underneath the blanket. This trick would only last for a while before someone noticed. At least it would give him a chance to perhaps clear his cob-webbed head. This would give him a fighting chance to escape, if only he knew where he was? It was a sound-proof building, no sounds would give Paul a clue to where he was; he would have to wing it.

Someone walked in, looked at the instruments on the wall, made a time check on the clipboard at the end of the bed; and then left. Paul began wiggling his toes, and then moved on to his feet. They ached, but the rust was coming off; all the bicycling seemed to actually be paying off, in the long run. Paul found he could look at the chrome circle around the clock on the wall that was directly in front of him. Any passerby could be seen in the chrome circle, then they seem to come into view. It was the only strategic option that he could find to try to plan anything.

There was no closet in the room that he could see, so Paul figured that he wouldn't have any luck trying to find his clothes. That meant he had to get something to wear, to get out of this white nightmare situation. Finding any clothes in this sanitary nightmare would be difficult. Paul began to disconnect himself from the multiple tubes, needles, and all the nightmare stuff that he feared as a child. It took him a while, because he was trying to move slowly and covertly; he may not get another chance to be conscious enough to escape!

Paul could feel an unusual attachment at the back of his skull, it was like nothing he had seen, or at least felt like ever before. It was back near the medulla area of his head; consisting of small "acupuncture" size needles, it took him the longest to disconnect it. Lastly, he relieved himself of the body fluid connections. He slowly slid down in the bed, to see if there were any other unknown attachments left for him to disconnect; or if he was truly free of it all. The sliding created a small blood-trail down the white sheets, that he couldn't do much about. It appeared that he had finally gotten free enough to make a break for it. He tilted his head to access how may doors, and the locations; he then looked for something to cause a distraction. On the far wall was a red handled, "Fire Alarm" that would do the trick.

He was putting together as much as he could as far as planning; but Paul knew this could be a futile effort, if seen he would be sedated instantly. Paul found some water and tried to soothe his sore throat. He then used the remaining plastic pitcher to wash and slick back his hair. He thought it might perhaps, disguise him enough not to be noticed. It was time to make a dash for the fire alarm; he fluffed his sheets, blankets, and pillow to be bulked up enough to look like someone might still be in the bed from hell.

His first step wasn't his best, as he fell to the floor and had to grab the I.V. stand to help him regain his stance. He took a few baby steps and began to feel his feet under him, it was a good feeling that just about made him cry. He was wondering what Cara must be thinking, she must be worried sick…he caught himself from falling and reminded himself to stay in the moment. He knew he couldn't afford to make too many mistakes; he would stay frosty.

There were about twenty yards to that bastard alarm, if someone were to come in unexpectedly; he would be busted! He decided there may be windows that he could be seen, so he would stay low, and hustle for it! Paul would simply try not to fall; that could create noise to be heard by others. He slowly cracked the door open, focusing on if there were any possible electric alarms on the door, but after a few seconds, he pushed it open and darted for the wall! He found a small metal waste basket along his way, he grabbed it and began stuffing items inside it. Filling it quickly as he rushed toward the alarm, Paul used the trash as a shield to hide his face. He got to the alarm successfully, and then pulled it down! Nothing happened! "What the hell?" he thought. It was a silent alarm apparently, so there would still be a response. He headed for the "door number one" and found it opened a small closet. There was a drop-cloth for painting inside, Paul took the center and brought it down hard on the door latch, it tore the fabric center, which allowed Paul to tear it further, creating a sort of poncho that he quickly put on.

He found some cleaning solvents, he tipped the jug enough to use about half a cup, covering the lower, right side of his new garment. Paul found some other bottles of non-flammable looking stuff that he covered the rest of his poncho. Now he knew where to ignite the low and right side, if he found any flame to ignite it. He had changed his appearance from a frail, bed-ridden man; he was carrying the trash, wearing a stained cloth, (that was now flammable). Paul found door number two, led to a hallway that had offices and cubicles connecting. No one seemed very alarmed yet, so the silent alarm must have been working. Paul moved quickly and with purpose, (and barefoot.)

Paul got to the end of the hallway and found a welcome "green" light that had the four-lettered word he wanted to see…" EXIT!" As he went through the door, it led to a stairwell, the number six was on the wall. "Crap," Paul thought to himself, "I have to go down five flights!" It would be the longest five-story set of stairs that Paul would ever deal with and the most memorable. It took him far too long, but he finally got the bottom, the cold concrete stairs and steel rails were frigid on his feet and hands. They hurt anyway, from him knocking away the invisible rust!

The bottom floor door opened slowly, as a crazy-looking, barefoot and homeless looking man crept out and onto the unknown street, in an unknown city. As soon as he saw four men dressed in black suits spin inside the lobby toward him; Paul began to try to move quicker – to freedom! He stumbled a bit and fell, not seeing the feet of an unknown man smoking a cigarette, in his designated space. Paul grabbed it and set his lower right bottom on fire! The man smoking began to yell, "You're on fire!" Paul kept moving and when the four men tried to abduct him, they found more than a fiery mass, moving quickly down the street. Paul finally broke free by leaving the men holding the flaming cloth! He turned into an alley and found a large trash container and he dove in it, hiding. The stench was bad, but the kidnapping would be worse. Paul stayed quiet until the dark overcome the day, and then he heard several people talking, but no one seemed to discover his location. He had time to think, awaken, and smell for quite some time.

NO ONE

"So that no one can buy or sell unless," the old book said;
   "He has the mark, the name of the beast or its name." it led
one to refer to nine numbers, instead of a name;
   nine numbers instead of a soul; it was a shame.

How could the dark of night,
  be so very white?
What hell allows no one to fight for life?
  A sleepy grave that cuts like a knife.

Fighting the light, bruised and battered,
  taking of a life that mattered…
A single man can only battle when he's awake,
  the world surrounding him, no choice to make.

Grasp the dry breath as if it were the last,
  reach down into your past…
Finding in your gut, the strength you need;
  to fight until you're freed!

Break the shackles that the world has born,
  fight for life that has been torn;
awaken, and survive to fight another day,
  in foggy sleep you cannot stay!

As your nine numbers are cast,
  how will you outlast?
Will you squander away,
  or fight, damn it, today!

Give unto Caesar, what belongs to him,
  put down nine numbers – again.
But live today to fight tomorrow,
  Do not leave loved ones in sorrow.

Within you is the power to heal.
  Pray to God you can still feel.
When you have nine numbers, but you're a one,
  within you is the strength….not to be done!

Chapter 16

The night had grown silent, the garbage had become ripe; the movement Paul continued to practice, was allowing him to regain use of his limbs. He peeped out of the garbage slowly, and cautiously, but he couldn't see much anyway. He formulated a plan to pull himself from the smell and slime that surrounded him. He did it as stealthy as he could, but it still made a little noise. He finally got to his feet, quickly hiding behind some other container. The fire-trick had worked, but it left it naked once again. He had found some trash bags that had been expendable, he dawned the garbage bag, punching a whole in the upside-down bottom, for his head, and then two arms sprung through; the classic look was complete.

As Paul shuffled from one alley to the cover of cars, to another street, and then he realized he was still in Portland. He had no intention of trying to make it back to his demolished rental room; but he knew the street people and that turned out to be a great investment. Paul had to hide under an SUV once, he knew if the police picked him up, he would be in Dr. Grey's hands shortly thereafter. At the end of an old Galaxy 500, was a familiar face, but it was the "new and improved" S-Phyliss. She looked healthy, she looked radiant, she looked sexy, she looked pregnant! She didn't recognize Paul, she shunned him; like the public was supposed to. He didn't look his best, but Paul knew his work that stood between a car and a stone rental building. As soon as Paul felt the shame, the pain, the emptiness of being homeless, he collapsed crying, "It's Paul…" The fallen angel picked Paul up and took him inside where he showered and had a meal provided for him. She introduced her new husband to Paul, they were old sweethearts. During the processing of Paul, she had found him, and that had led to happiness and pregnancy! As soon as she returned with a burner cell phone, Paul was anxious to check on Cara via the family.

His Uncle Don picked up the phone and answered the mystery number that was being presented. He took a lot of crank calls, shopping calls, and took too many surveys by answering that damn phone. But it finally paid off.

"Uncle Don," Paul quickly inserted, "It's me Paul!"

"Where the hell have you been kid," Uncle Don queried, "we haven't heard from you in about six months!"

"It's a long story Uncle Don," Paul wanted to get to the heart of the conversation, "where is Cara, is she safe, is she still in Seneca?" The Eastern Oregon town was more than a haven, many found sanctuary there.

"Yea, kiddo, she's certainly safe, but she was worried sick, she went to Portland several times just to drive around and try to find you!" Don advised. She isn't here right now, she went to town with your Aunt; but you need to get your ass home son!"

"I plan on doing that," Paul agreed, "but I may need to go to Coos Bay before I can meet up with Cara. Let her know I'm okay now, tell her to stay there and be safe".

Uncle Don asked some questions of Paul, but he didn't get much answers to things Paul wouldn't discuss over the phone. The call ended quickly as to not draw attention in case someone was monitoring the cell towers. At least his family was alright, but it seemed like Dr. Grey owed Paul six months of his life! The debt that all men pay; lingered in Paul's mind briefly. Cara would not be happy about staying put, but she would be happy that Paul had finally gotten an opportunity to let her know he was alive.

The normal hustle and bustle of Portland was now explosive; the media growth after The Healing in the child burn unit seemed to intensify the city. Paul was staying with Phyliss and Steve, (and Elizabeth, when she arrived.) He had to eat some real food, gain some strength, and prepare to plan a trip to Coos Bay still. While watching the TV, he had the opportunity to watch the DVR recordings of news that Phyliss had recorded regarding the "Angel of Death".

"Why do they call it that?" Paul asked, with hurt in his voice. "Angel of Death" refers to taking life, why is the media spinning it like that?" Paul asked Phyliss.

"I guess," Phyliss reasoned, "they think death follows you, wherever you go there is people hurt or dying."

"Yes," Paul pleaded, "but you know…there has been life, and healing of people."

"You don't have to explain it to me," Phyliss interjected, "Paul, you have me a second chance on life that I can never repay or thank you enough, I'm on your side!" She went to Paul and comforted him on the couch, hugging his tears away.

The story in the news seemed to bend the truth, certainly lie about what had happened, but they were making such broad strokes of a lie that the public was paying money for it. A local hate group had posted a reward for anyone that assaulted Paul, "The Angel of Death". Certain channels didn't seem to elaborate much on the story. One recorded interview with a prominent member of a church, made references of Saint Paul. They persuaded the public that there is no person out there, they believed it was only a reoccurrence of Saint Paul, since many street people confirmed that it was "Paul" helping them.

One tabloid that Phyliss picked up, depicted a dark "Angel of Death" and actually made a reference to the ugly artist conception, as St. Paul. It was impossible for Paul to imagine why the city had grown to believe such hateful lies. It was as if money was perhaps funding this fake news. Paul only knew one person that would probably go for such a dirty way of doing business. Dr. Grey was not all that innocent, Paul was beginning to wonder about the agenda of WHIP too.

Most of the city had started to forget about the children in the burn unit about two or three months after it had occurred. Interestingly enough, the three children, "Malcom, Amy, and Charles" began returning to the burn center – every Thursday, of every month, praying and visiting their friends that were still victims of fire within the ward. This upset the norm, media, and their families; but the children could never forget The Healing! They believed in the wonder and left science and family pressure behind. Paul finally figured out that he must have visited the kids on a Thursday and if he were to confirm their faith, he would creep in on a Thursday.

Two weeks later, Paul, Phyliss, and Steve were going through the familiar doors of the children's burn unit. They were posing as family, Steve apparently was pretty good at finding information on computers to make it handy. The security was a little tighter, there was some presenting of false identifications involved. The trio had a bit of a plan and were determined to help a handful of kids. They were intent on throwing a monkey wrench into the media that kept dogging Paul. Paul grabbed a white lab coat that was hanging on the back of a chair, along the way to the same floor that Paul had visited over six months before.

Steve shook his finger at Paul, in a "don't steal" motion, when he saw the lab coat lifted by Paul off the chair. Paul donned the garment and simply said, "Don't argue with the Doc!" The group rounded the corner at the end of the hall and found a Nurse Station; the group planned on avoiding staff, so it took them by surprise, when Paul headed bravely toward the station, instead of hiding.

"Doctor Steven," Paul lied, "you have got to see the progress on this burn victim," he then looked up at the nurse and advised they would be at the end of the hall in the last room on the left. The nurse hardly looked up, stating something like, "let me know if you need anything." At the designated room, that had been picked purely at random, was a small infant that was the result of being left in a car, which had also had an engine fire. The result was probably quadriplegic.

Two accomplices kept watch while Paul began to rub the stubby limbs with his finger, (his hand would have been too big.) Steve was looking over his shoulder as he witnessed an infant that quit crying and began cooing. Slowly, five small buds began to push out from within, and tiny fingers and toes were beginning to grow! Steve began crying, he couldn't help it.

Paul whispered, "My work here is done, let's go to the next room" and the trio proceeded to the next room that was beside their previous. The next child's name was Paul, this disturbed Paul a little, but he was the victim of a chemical burn to the chest. It almost had made his chest translucent, and there was still the smell that couldn't be forgotten by the group. After Paul introduced himself as Paul, the eight-year-old boy was genuinely thankful to make a friend.

Paul asked Paul if he could touch his chest and say a small prayer for the child. The child was in no condition to deny anything, but there was a positive nod. Paul began praying, as his friends were keeping watch, Steve had regained his composure. Within two minutes the boy named Paul was standing to thank Paul. He agreed to hide in the bed and room for a few minutes, although the little boy wouldn't let go of the firm embrace that held Paul tightly. The boy was crying, Steve was crying again, and now it was Phyliss who broke into tears.

They exited the room, Paul felt tugging at his chest and heart a little bit. Maybe the six months had taken its toll on him, more than he realized. He started to stagger a bit, Steve caught him as Phyliss asked if he was okay. Paul motioned the group forward and the cadre moved to the next room. There was a teenage girl that had lost half of her hair and the same side of her face to fire. Paul didn't want to know how it happened, but he asked her politely if he could hold her hand, (she would not allow him near her head.)

Paul held her hand and began praying, the two keeping watch had regained their composure a little, but each child expressed love, affection, pain, hopelessness, and courage, differently. Within a couple minutes, The Healing had begun to change a formless, charred, child's face into rosy cheeks and corn silk-golden hair was beginning to flow. Paul couldn't help crying a little, Charity saw the tears. She reached up and dried Paul's tear. A hug followed that took too long. The two at the door motioned Paul and grabbed at his white lab coat. The nurse's rounds were calling for her to check her patients.

Paul stumbled and had to be helped by the other two to exit via the available avenue, circling around the nurse, so she never saw them make the full circle and exit. He had some pains in his chest now that were never present when he was healing children before. The group made it down safely, discarding the white lab coat in the fire stairwell; they exited as the visitors, right on time. Within a couple minutes, the alarms began…Paul imagined they weren't loud, screaming, alarms; they were heavenly angels singing, they were proud – and loud! Steve was a good egg; he began speaking to the other two, (now) fugitives, "Why would the wonderful effects of healing – demand they set off alarms?" No one – knew the answer.

Chapter 17

After Paul had rested up, acquired some funds for travel, via a wire transfer to Steve; he was about ready for travel again. Paul had told his partner, Dick Spencer, that he would be returning…he never imagined it would be over a half year later. After using his gift, to give Dick another chance at life; Paul didn't feel as though Dick owed him anything. He was a good partner, the two had grown the veterinary clinic on the coast together. Paul felt as though he had abandoned his partner. The doubling of the workload onto one person – especially without prior notice, was too much.

Dick was a kind soul, he probably hired a temp, with no identified end date. Paul didn't think that he could return to Coos Bay, return to the clinic, return to work, and act like nothing had happened. He was feeling better, and he knew that his old life was only a vast, happy, and routine, memory. The future was certainly always in God's hands. Paul wished he was in Cara's arms.

When Cara received the news, she did just about what Paul anticipated; she borrowed a relative's vehicle to drive to Coos Bay. Regretfully, Dr. Grey was a step ahead; after the children's burn unit incident. It was almost like a slap in the face to WHIP, they were receiving blood tests and brain activity reports on Paul from the hidden lab. They certainly believed that they had the "Paul" situation handled by Dr. Grey. The corporate trust in Dr. Grey was wobbling a bit, especially since the number of cured burn unit victims had now doubled! Meetings were being held; some Dr. Grey attended, some were skyped, some made sure that he wasn't in attendance. There seemed to be a few secrets that WHIP wasn't telling Dr. Grey, and Dr. Grey wasn't telling everything he knew; Paul knew he would not fall victim to the "White Fog" of medical testing – ever again.

There were four men in black that intercepted Cara as she was refueling, (two counties away from Seneca.) The men had placed her in zip-tie restraints, covered her head with a black hood, (that didn't allow her to view anything) and then tucked her into the trunk of the governmental looking black sedan. Dr. Grey was getting desperate, but not fool-hearty, he had sent four goons for one girl; taking no chances. This time, he would not underestimate this veterinarian, he knew if he could control the love in his heart, Grey could control Paul.

Cara found that breathing was difficult, her heart was racing! Because she was naturally frightened, the confined space, and the hood; required Cara to calm herself. She realized this and began counting to one hundred. By the time she reached the one hundred beers on the wall, she had calmed down, slowed her breathing, and began to realize her environment.

She knew that all newer vehicles have a trunk release within the trunk, in the form of a button. The restraints and the hood made it impossible for her to do any magic trick escape. She reasoned that the two barriers in front of her goal had to be dealt with first, in order for her to prepare for an escape.

She could feel the hinge post where the trunk lid sealed; she knew that it's edge may prove accessible from her angle of restraint. She started rubbing the restraint against the small metal surface, (that she could only imagine, since it was behind her back). Slowly and carefully, she began to put pressure on the plastic by expanding her wrists against each other.

Snap! The restraint pulled apart, it jolted Cara a little, making some noise that she hoped the idiots in the back seat, (just mere inches away) didn't hear the ruckus. She then completed the other hurdle of removing the damn hood! Now she was ready for these turds that have tried to come between her and her veterinarian! As the vehicle probably had a light that would indicate an open trunk, if Cara pushed the yellow button that she located. She decided that with the speed of the vehicle, it would keep the trunk closed, but the light would give away her advantage of surprise. It was difficult, but she knew she would have to make her move whenever the vehicle slowed or stopped. It would be a sign of population and fleeing safely.

Waiting about an hour, it seemed like an eternity. Finally, the vehicle began slowing, the men were talking, some was distinguishable, they were going to stop for fuel and check on their cargo. The black vehicle pulled slowly into the fueling station, Cara was ready to spring like a cougar. She waited for the first "ding" that would be caused by the front tires crossing the pressure line, to indicate to the attendant a vehicle was arriving.

The ding was like a shot at a swim meet! Cara pushed the button, with the vehicle still moving, but coming to a halt. The red light on the dash indicated the trunk was open, but the driver was addressing his passengers and didn't quite see it yet. In a single flowing motion, Cara held on to the lid as she swung it open and then rolled backward, away from the black bastard vehicle! She continued rolling like a log down the hill, almost too far, since there was another car that had to hit the brakes to avoid hitting her!

Cara got up and began running, not turning around, not looking back, not apologizing to the driver that almost hit her! She continued running into a small shopping plaza that was apparently part of the fueling station too. She couldn't take the chance of the men seeing her, pursuing her, and using any false identification to appear like law enforcement or government. She would not be re captured! As soon as she found the front row of cars parked for convenience food nearby, she looked for a vehicle that was unlocked. She finally found an old Caprice wagon, climbed into the back and covered herself with anything that she could in the back, and then tried to control her breathing and heart that was racing!

She knew that first place they would search would be the female bathrooms, but as the owner came out and got into the old station wagon, backed out – pulling out onto the freeway; Cara was breathing better already. She would travel wherever this vehicle driver would take her and then bail out later, hopefully taking a bus would be less conspicuous. She rested, waited, and wondered where this free ride would end.

Riding in the back of the escape vehicle, Cara began putting this puzzle together in her head. She realized there were some people with money and power trying desperately to kidnap her or Paul, or both. It was upsetting, but now she was a bit more aware of the danger that may lay ahead. Cara's love would be her guiding light. She would use her "Tomboy" instincts and get to the heart of this mess. She would protect Paul, she would show him that she was not without abilities; just not heavenly, like his! Secretly, she worried about Paul; she knew he had a kind heart, she worried that it might just be a bit too much for his heart. It was certain that if he had used his ability, it was taking a toll on Paul. She wanted to help him understand it, but she really would like him to be cautious enough to curb – or even stop the use if it was killing him. The conversations that she would have with her lover, were being rehearsed in her head as her heart was calling for her to "Charge Forward" to protect him!

Cara was charging forward, in reverse. The unsolicited ride, (that she needed at the time) was speeding toward the driver's destination – Ontario, Oregon. It was almost in the exact opposite direction that Cara needed to go toward Coos Bay. When the vehicle stopped at a Post Office, to gather the drivers mail; Cara bailed. It took her about five minutes to get her bearing; the good thing, was that no one would be looking for her here! The city of

Ontario was just on the border of Oregon and Idaho. A quick freeway jaunt, and you were in Idaho. There was a lot of long-haul truckers headed from Boise, Idaho to the Oregon Coast. Cara found a very nice trucker in a nearby Rest Area that had been sleeping off a double haul. She told the elder trucker, that she was the daughter of the Coos Bay Chief of Police. She really sold it, when she said her last name, and knew that it was a female Chief! No fast moves by the driver, Cara only observed cruise control speed limits.

It was going to be an "all day" haul, taking about ten or eleven hours; the trucker promised to behave himself if Cara was going to nod off and take a nap. Knowing that he could finally drive faster and make some time; the trucker also knew he could be arrested if he touched the young woman. Sleep did not come easy, it wasn't ever easy for Cara to sleep in a car; much less a big rig hauler. The vibration, jostling, and humming finally rocked Cara to sleep and she was able to dream of anything; except the last days events.

She awoke startled a little bit, probably still half in a dream, but she let out a bit of a nervous, response, that only her dream would know why. The nervous driver began to try and whistle nervously, like nothing had happened. There was a scent of a sweaty seat cushion, some inexpensive after shave, and dust. Cara sneezed the memory of the dream out – via a loud, "Aww-Chew!"

The driver quickly said, "Bless You!" and added they would be near Reedsport, which was less than an hour away from Coos Bay. Reedsport is a wonderful community that was the first coastal city that would connect to the historical Oregon 101 highway, along the entire coast. Cara advised this would be close enough, since she wanted to phone her Mother, to come and pick her up – hitchhiking was prohibited in the family. The driver seemed to understand, promising he would not tell anyone…just what Cara wanted from the conversation. She was coy, or clever, or both.

She wanted to drop by an ATM but knew better. She had some cash that would get her by, but she also knew the credit card use was going to be untouchable. Cara's coworker lived in Reedsport, near the golf course. Cara made her way to her friends, she knew that she was unexpected, uninvited, and unanticipated. Joice was that kind of friend that would probably make her lunch, loan her money, and rent a car for her! Cara only hoped she could catch her at home, hopefully her work schedule hadn't changed.

After a very nice soup and sandwich, Joice prepared Cara for her trip, (that she knew nothing about, hadn't seen her, and wouldn't be discussing at work.) The workings of the veterinarian clinic were discussed a bit before Cara would catch the casino bus to Coos Bay. It helped to know what had been going on in her absence. It sounded as though they had hired some temps from Coquille to cover the absences of both Paul and Cara. It was comforting to know that they could cover; but it was a bit sad that they could be replaced easily if needed. Cara was certain that if she laid low, used caution, and restricted knowledge of her location; she could blend in on the coast. After all, she was a Gold Beach girl!

There were about twenty friends of Cara's, but her inner circle consisted of about five that could be trusted with her life. It would be these five best friends that she would play hopscotch with, always moving about. She would listen to the local news, read the local papers, and try to filter what was real, from the rest. It was almost a guess, but Cara knew that Paul would surface, and when she was needed, she would swoop in – and save her lover!

Paul could tend to get himself into trouble, but he had a knack for pulling something out of a hat too. Cara believed that *she*…was the best thing to pull out of a hat! She was a little cleverer than these guys were counting on. After stopping by the friend that ran one of the local pawn shops, Cara picked up a CO_2 pistol that looked real, except for the red tip that she cut off. She now had a legal handgun that might pass for a real firearm if she used it in a pinch. It probably would get someone's attention if she hit their face or ears too.

She found a metal, decorative belt; it had little simulated turquoise in the middle of each of the many sections that all linked together. Cara took a file to several of the links in the back, sharpening them so very sharp, she had to thread her belt loops carefully to wear the thing. Now if someone were to try to grab her around the waste, she knew how to spin and cut! She then honed a couple links to cut the plastic wrist restraints. She would not be bound again by anyone!

Cara would also carry a couple of simulated blood capsules, (just in case she wanted to look wounded – or make someone else) they fit perfectly into her little aspirin, pill case. Lastly, she had a small belt buckle that hid a concealed blade. She felt equipped to fight for her man; hopefully she could be there for him.

Chapter 18

It took Paul longer than usual to heal up, gather his strength, and begin the final ascent to feeling good again. Just like age; it seemed to take a bit longer to heal – it took longer each time. Paul noticed, but dismissed the idea. He was more intrigued by the news media on the television. The important people were all making statements on the squawk-box, that three child victims were kidnapped from the medical center. They didn't mention the three releases that occurred, just hours before.

Blatant lies were filling the air waves! It was confusing to Paul; "How would they even be able to prove these lies to the newspapers?" he wondered. Most newspapers would be following the story on the television, or perhaps it was just the opposite. It was sheer madness to him, Steve and Phyliss were wanting to act; but Paul let them know that was exactly what would reveal their location. There was some wanted posters and media with pictures of Paul; someone was working with the Feds, Law Enforcement, and even the media. This only clarified that the Grey matter was to surely blame.

With so very much *disinformation* flying everywhere, it was almost impossible for the public to see through the smoke-screen. It was disheartening to Paul, it made him want to stand on top of the Rose City's water tower and scream the truth; at least throw some expletives toward some people! The early morning fog that seemed to settle in Portland was also a fog of deceit, lies, and purchased media; too much – to thick, today.

Perhaps it was the ugly lies of fake news that fueled Paul's recovery. He began to work-out physically, walking a lot on the treadmill, but he also practiced some calisthenics to focus his body more. Paul realized he could *nothing* about Dr. Grey, he could only control his actions and response. Yoga seemed to compliment the process; soon he thanked Steve and Phyliss for all their help and he wished them a very happy and healthy baby!

He caught a train, then a bus to a casino on the coast, he would then borrow a friend's car and make his way down to Coos Bay via the beautiful 101. Some of the highway had been mud-washed, (slides occur due to the rain) some sections were always under repair, but as long as it wasn't closed

– Paul would be golden. His plan worked well until he hit the small town of Granger; as he slowed the vehicle, (due to an accident and EMS on site) the local Douglas County deputy motioned him to pull to the side and join the que of vehicles already pulled over.

Paul cruised to the side in his friend's economy commuter; the overweight deputy was headed down to speak to vehicles, friendly chatting with each driver of the five cars before Paul. As he reached Paul, his friendly grin begged for the window to be opened. Paul touched a lever and the window buzzed down, without a single stall in a smooth motion, the deputy laid his left arm on the car door, moved his right arm in, and a needle that Paul never saw…hushed him to sleep. The drivers of the other cars simply signaled back into traffic; a large and jovial man that was a deputy before – now wore a sweatshirt, driving the vehicle with Paul asleep in the seat-belted passenger seat. The group whisked up some signs and left a stolen ambulance with lights flashing.

Cruising to a location unknown to everyone, (except the lead vehicle) the group of various drivers were trained to drive erratically if any real law enforcement were to approach the last two tail vehicles – containing Paul and Cara. The bandits would then lead a merry chase to distract the real value targets at the tail. It was an old trick, but it often worked. Neither Paul or Cara were conscious enough to know the location of each other; and yet, they were being reunited.

At a very beautiful house, purchased by someone very famous for their mother; the Coos Bay couple would not know the house had no public access. It was hidden well, from the public, media, and any peering eyes. It could definitely be seen from the water however; Paul awoke, (thanking God he wasn't hooked up to any medical equipment) staring at the water. He wasn't sure if his captors knew he was awake, so he cautiously looked at anything in the room that had a reflection; thereby seeing behind him.

The sliding, or gliding, glass doors facing the water allowed a slight reflection of a sofa behind Paul, with someone on it. He decided to simply roll – like a rug, away from the sofa toward the doors. This would put distance between the kidnapper and the rug roller! Not positive about his feet, but if they were bound, it wouldn't prohibit the roll. Paul began to count down in his head, reaching the one finally, he quickly rolled exactly as planned, away from Cara. She was on the sofa, still out from the damn drugs!

Paul sprang up, (to find his feet were not bound) and bolted toward Cara like a flash to check her physically. She seemed alright, no injuries, (but some slight pressure marks on her wrists, where she must have been restrained.) Paul couldn't imagine someone trying to restrain her, Cara was strong, independent, and could wrestle an animal for any necessity. Paul thought to himself, "Oh yea, Cara kicked like a horse, some guy had frozen peas on his sack, after dealing with her!"

"Oh, crap!" Cara bolted awake, sitting up, "Paul!" she realized, launching into his arms! "You won't believe what I've been going through!" Cara offered, "It's been crazy, and a close friend sold me out, damn it!"

"I know sweetie," Paul consoled, as he began kissing her and hugging her uncontrollably. It was secretly a confirmation to Paul that she was alive, and well; he wondered how far Dr. Grey would go, including what might happen to Cara.

Cara asked the ultimate question, "So where in the heck are we?" She followed with a barrage of follow up elephants in the room; "Do you know who did this, was it that Dr. Grey dude, what if it's someone else, like the government?" She took a breath and then continued, "You know, it takes money to break the law, that's what this is you know, it's illegal; hello – kidnapping?"

Paul saw his opening, so he went for it; "I distinctly remember hearing us cross the McCullough Memorial Bridge…so we're in Coos Bay or North Bend, you can't mistake crossing that bridge". At least the two knew they had to be in Coos County; they knew their stomping grounds well.

"As for who is responsible; we'll just have to see who brings our food, while we try to explore our surroundings," Paul surmised. "I just think that Grey would have me hooked up to something; at the very least, he would be taking more blood," Paul took another guess. Cara leaned over, as if to whisper something in case the room was bugged, "You are so sexy when you're making sense to my questions!"

The two companions were like PB & J, they seem to complement each other, it was good to be a team once again. Cara had a perspective that Paul never seem to grasp, but she liked the comfort she would feel, when feeling uneasy, or frightened, when Paul would respond to her. As the duo split up to canvas the room, they began searching for cameras or listening devices. It seemed like a good idea, usually the smaller the bug, the more it costs. These would be a bit difficult to find; since their host was willing to commit assault, kidnapping, and a whole host of other laws, money was apparent.

It was not a hospital room, it had a nice view of the water, appeared to be private, and the room seemed like something out of a magazine. Someone was very comfortable; the two explorers had no idea that the house was owned by the mother of a famous celebrity. It probably wouldn't have made much of a difference; the true owner probably didn't even know he or she had house guests. Paul made a point not to tell Cara that the owner may be reported missing…it was an unbearable thought, but not past the lawless critter's deeds.

Cara made a point to misdirect Paul from the same thoughts that he was already thinking about the possible deceased owner, "So, they should be bringing us food and something to drink?"

Paul smiled at the effort, knowing he missed that about her. Cara would look into the ugly mess of an animal that needed caring for; and smile invitingly, it was almost as if she was saying, "C'mon in, the waters fine!" There was one delivery of a calf that was breach, Paul thought her look was crazy at the time! But she dove right in like a trooper. That was another thing that Paul liked about her, she wasn't afraid to do what was necessary.

No camera could be found, no listening bugs either; which only meant they were too small or too cleverly placed. The two would have kept looking, but they were pleasantly surprised by a maid delivering room service, (the food smelled good, and Paul didn't think it was drugged, but it wouldn't be the first time.)

Paul advised Cara not to eat it, just to be on the safe side, but the small woman that delivered it smiled, she asked warmly if she could sample the food to make sure it was at temperature. Paul simply said yes, and the lady began tasting a small fork of this and that; finally; Paul thanked her and simply advised that the food would be fine. The two ate with no consequence. It was prepared by a professional chef, tasted great, and was large portions. Paul really enjoyed having dinner with his lover; it had been a while. They weren't sure how long this would last, but they would enjoy the moment with each other as much as possible.

The bottle of *Columbia Crest* was finished by the two; they at least felt warm, comfortable, sated, and safe for the moment; which was exactly what their captors wanted. A previously unnoticed light turned on and off at the top of a bookcase near the door. It was accompanied by an audible trill that seem to be serving in unison with the light as a doorbell. Paul and Cara both looked at each other, wondering what would happen next. Yet, nothing occurred. The two captives looked at each other again, Cara finally spoke up, "Come in!"

A very distinguished man in an uncomfortably expensive, silk suit used a key and the door electronically unlocked, as the man stepped in, he closed the door behind him, "Hello Paul and Cara," he began the introduction, "my name is Corrie, I'll be serving as your Liaison while you're here." He explained that he served at the will of a very wealthy family that preferred not to be known. He also advised that they were in no danger, although for their own safety, they would remain captive in the luxurious room for now. There were lots of questions that Paul and Cara needed answers to; they had little choice in the presence of an employee of their captors, they nodded and appeared agreeable.

The two generally acted and thought in unison, they simply looked at each other and knew that they would wait until the well-dressed man left, they would begin to hatch an escape plan. Cara asked if they would be drugged again, or if it was safe to eat and drink what was provided. Corrie assured them that he believed they needed the two to be healthy and alert, to make their own decisions when the "offer" was presented.

The statement was both assuring, but also concerning to the captives. Lastly, Paul asked when any remaining questions would be answered, Corrie said they were planning on him having a meeting that afternoon, when the first hurdle of communication was introduction. Paul had little choice to agree, he asked for a menu to order from; instead of relying of what was served, (he advised Corrie that Cara didn't eat onions – in any form.)

The first meeting seemed to go according to Corrie's plan, the two were at least willing to talk, and rapport was the first thing that he needed to establish. He also realized the suspicious minds of hostages are usually always focused on escape. Corrie was no fool, it was why he was called in on this one. He was expensive, but worth it usually.

The two in the confinement room would believe he was FBI, CIA, or NSA, or some other damn acronym; which would make his job tougher. He would need to shed his title, become familiar with them; use his active listening skills to reason with their likes and avoid the triggers that would bring dislike, or mistrust. He had been to all the training, Corrie was good at his job.

Chapter 19

The meeting that followed later between the three of them was cordial but cutting like a knife too. Corrie had certain issues that he could not bend, but anything else was on the table for discussion. Primarily, Paul and Cara were kidnapped to protect them from WHIP; but this large, unknown and well-funded group, were researchers on the Bird Fire epidemic. They had continued to investigate, document, and research clues that were only now emerging.

Paul liked the fact that they didn't have some acronym for a name, (like WHIP) but he didn't trust them anymore than the others that had taken him hostage earlier. Whomever was paying for all this, was well connected and funded; but most importantly, they had intelligence gathered from around the world, (and especially the Northwest.)

Cara and Paul were feeling like they were at one of those "free weekend vacation seminars" they were forced to listen to a presentation by Corrie that was informative, but boring. Until he mentioned the small factoid at the conclusion of the two-and-a-half-hour presentation, "So, to sum it up," Corrie sounded like a used car salesman, "the after-effects of the Bird Fire, is causing sterility in men at an alarming rate, some countries report possible entire sterility in ten years."

Cara woke up from the boring daze; "Wait, did you just say what I think you said; is the world becoming sterile?" Cara had now bitten into this and wasn't going to let go, "Is this going to happen to everyone, am I at risk, what about women?" Paul knew that there would follow a barrage of questions, in a single breath. "What about the US, compared to other countries," she began, "who's working on this, shouldn't the rest of the country know this, by whose authority do you have to not tell the public, and another thing…" Thank goodness, Corrie finally interrupted to answer some of her questions, Cara got to catch a breath.

"Hey," the smooth talker began, "I've got family too, you know!" He looked sincere and caring, he was perfect, "I have a father, and a son; that I would like to see have children of his own for God's sake!" Even a crack in his voice, Corrie was using the Stockholm Syndrome in his favor, trying to humanize himself, to gain their rapport. Paul wasn't sure if Corrie was sincere, if he was lying, or if he just wanted to shut Cara up!

"Look," Paul finally spoke after listening to Cara's concerns, and Corrie's sale for trust, "if you were kidnapped… and your hostage-taker was to tell you something," Paul leaned forward, looking at Corrie into his eyes, "why would you trust a damn thing they said?" Paul knew he made a valid point, so he pounded the last like a coffin-nail, "Until you show good faith and release us immediately, we will never trust you or believe anything you say; if your name really is Corrie".

The well-dressed man stood up, (as if insulted) he smiled and said he understood, "I'll quit the charade as your Liaison and take up my role as your host!" He smiled again and laughed under his breath, "I am your host you know, this is my home." Then with a bit louder voice he spoke, "Ultra!" and the locks all clicked open. "Our home is your home," Corrie said.

"This is actually," Corrie began, "a place owned by a celebrity that is shooting a film in Uzbekistan, he bought it for his mother, but she's deceased." He continued to talk as he walked out the open door, "We have made it comfortable, but also very secure; CCTV and microwave monitoring system everywhere," Corrie concluded, "I need you both to believe me, long enough to see the reports and footage we have compiled here."

Cara was already getting up to follow the talking guy, Paul was ready to make his move too. They both looked very concerned and began to exit the room to assess rooms and exits. There appeared to be something to this bull that Corrie was shoveling, Paul just wasn't sure what his and Cara's role would be. It was easy to believe some of what Corrie was saying to possibly be true, but both Paul and Cara both had the feeling that he wasn't being fully truthful in his disclosure. They both seem to want to take it all in, filter it as info from a kidnapper, and then stock up supplies and make a break for it.

Corrie would be showing more information and cramming it down their throats until they got the hell out of there; Paul would pick up some of the intelligence for later review and use. Paul thought he would test "Corrie's system" with a question, "Hey, Corrie, do you know anything, or have any records of a Portland gangster shooting recently?"

Paul was surprised when Corrie shook his head in the affirmative, "The gangster that was shot, killed, and then resurrected by you?" Corrie could see the surprise in Paul's face, it seemed to scream, "Hey, how the hell did he know about that!" Cara stopped everything she was doing, "What the hell is he talking about?" Before she could bombard him with more concerns and questions, Paul took the initiative to hold his hands up defensively. He shook his head toward Cara, meaning to silently say, "Don't talk in front of the kidnapper!"

"I'm sure I don't know what you're talking about," Paul lied, "I was asking about a close friend of mine, he knew the deceased."

"Okay, I get it," Corrie smiled, "can't confirm or deny that it occurred" he turned and demonstrated that another door was unlocked, and another, "you see, I trust you with the house, and I trust you with the intelligence we've gathered." Corrie walked over to stand near Cara, "We won't discuss it further than this tidbit I must tell you; the gangster has turned a new leaf, serves as the Religious Services assistant, while incarcerated. He also apparently saved a man in jail who was hanging up in the same cell."

The three in the room weren't speaking in response to what was said, but Cara gave Paul the "You have some explaining to do Lucy! look." They took most of the day asking questions, eating some lunch, (stashing some fruit and bread for the breakout.) Corrie concluded their day by showing them the indoor swimming pool that had a wonderful view of the ocean through large accordion-folding glass panels. It was a stunning house, Paul wanted to see the basement, he seemed to believe it might be there that they may discover what Corrie was hiding – which may lead them to see through his friendship to see what his real reason for holding them. Paul and Cara knew they were in a gilded-cage; they would need to take their escape planning serious.

Corrie was cordial, but there was a hidden factor that the two couldn't figure. The research that was provided, could have been fabricated; but everything looked legitimate. There were health organizations that had accumulated data, world organizations were becoming aware of the increased amount of male impotency since the Bird Fire erupted. Scientists that were familiar with bird-born disease, scientists on migratory patterns, and even National Disaster was getting involved. The possibility of isolating the infection rate was simply too late. Most countries should have quarantined, isolated incoming and outgoing air flights, and involved CDC and Homeland Security in the beginning. They didn't anticipate the sterility as an after-effect, the world was obviously unprepared, playing catch-up would be the effort now.

Paul and Cara were finding some validity and truth, it seemed obvious that there was a possible world-wide threat; but their personal safety and escape would need to be the personal priority. They would have to be on their own to figure out what the next step would be; but they would not be held, (even in the beautiful gilded cage.)

Cara noticed the fault in the security perimeter that Paul had missed; the house could be exited, and the perimeter could be breached; by using a sheet tied into a loop, then thrown like a lasso; the flagpole could be grabbed with the sheet, and then use it like a swing rope over the fence and microwave to exit and flee the area.

Paul would cause a distraction, while Cara made the move with the sheet to jump to freedom. Corrie had no idea that the two were wanting to escape, since they told him they realized the data was valid; and the threat of global sterilization was a possible apocalyptic event. The plan was set on a Thursday the following week, and the two would spring loose. Paul was healing up pretty good, but Corrie was nudging him to prepare for some blood tests, and some screening, (as soon as he felt up to it.)

Cara would make sure that Paul was never up to it; she had been stashing food and supplies for an exit; the sheet was removed, (she used the top sheet, because a bottom fitted sheet would stretch possibly too far when they planned on swinging. The stage was set for their breakout. Corrie seemed a little suspicious lately, Cara and Paul believed that he was waiting for a VIP to impress, he seemed to try to put together data to impress someone, and he continued to mention important visitors that would love to meet Paul.

Paul had no desire to meet any doctors, or VIP's, he would have his hands full avoiding WHIP and Dr. Grey; he really didn't want to add to the list of people to avoid, (especially if they were hunting him and Cara.) He knew that his partner, Dick Spencer had just about given up on him and he worried about the business, his investment as a partner, he had concerns about his family, and then there was the issue that he may be sterile like everyone else; Cara would be heartbroken.

As they prepared the make-shift rope, made of the sheet, Cara got into position to throw the lasso and connect with the flagpole. She threw the sheet several times before she finally connected, and the sheet encircled the pole. She quickly pulled it tight and began tightening the escape device by leaning backward, putting weight onto the sheet-rope. Paul went into the lab area and climbed up onto a counter. He then used a small lighter that he had found, hidden, and smuggled; he lit the fire-suppression sprinkler. The result was the instant fire alarm and sprinklers being set off.

He left the area as quickly as possible, headed toward his lover and her escape device. There was a small staff response to the fire alarm, but the tech people were scrambling as much as Paul and Cara. As Paul reached the rendezvous point, he could hear people's voices yelling, there was chaos, which was just what was needed.

Cara believed it necessary for Paul to escape first, since there was no medical value of her; she demanded Paul go first, (to test the rope and ensure he made it first.) Paul grabbed the sheet and launched himself forward from the high point of the roof. He glided well, and the sheet rope did not fail.

Cara found herself waiting for Paul to throw the sheet back to her; waiting for her to swing into motion. It took several attempts for Paul to get the sheet back, as he finally exerted all the force he could to throw it back to her. Cara grabbed the sheet and as she began to swing; a shot rang out, she fell just on the other side of the fence. She had suffered a bullet wound, Paul grabbed her up and helped to move her away from the house and perimeter! They scrambled as quick as they could. There were voices yelling, alarms blaring, and Paul was almost carrying Cara.

As they reached the top of the hill, they found a paved road that led to the highway. Hurrying as fast as he could, Paul helped Cara get to the road. Cara finally demanded Paul put her down. Paul tried to place pressure on the chest wound that had been caused by the bullet entering the back and going out the chest. Cara looked up and said she loved Paul, she then expired from the fatal gunshot, and fell into Paul's arms. When it came to

Cara…there weren't any rules of use; The Healing would be needed now, more than ever…Paul was weeping and shaking uncontrollably.

Paul was beyond help, he couldn't leave her and flag a vehicle, but he knew it wasn't an option – he reached down to the love of his life and began praying, he then rubbed his warm hands over the wound and the blood receded. The gunshot began to turn red and yellow, finally it bruised and then the wound healed in the front, her back-injury area began to glow slightly – healing as Paul expected!

Cara slowly opened her eyes, as they filled with tears! She did not beat death, but it did not grasp her as Paul had interceded once again. This time was different in so very many ways; Paul loved Cara so very much that he couldn't bear to lose her. But as the rest of the world lost their loved ones in that single heartbeat. People in Europe, in a terrible catastrophic act of cowardice; a weak man broke up couples in love…tearing them apart with a speeding vehicle.

In the Orient a torrential flash flood demanded that two lovers be separated by a wall of water, that the husband barely escapes. Elsewhere in other countries, lovers were separated at the very instant that Paul laid hands on Cara! Regretfully, there was no "Paul" there for them; they were torn apart; only to be reunited later in their own religious after-life! God has many names, and he knew the names of the hundreds that died that day, as he allowed Cara to live.

Chapter 20

The state newspaper was fed some lies about a "Bonnie & Clyde" story of two drug-crazed individuals, that had burglarized a private residence, murdered some private security guard, and set fire to the lab; resulting in a full emergency response. The pictures of the two maniacs also advised they were armed and dangerous. The law enforcement community would be on the look-out, but so would the public. It was fortunate that Cara still had some true friends that would come to her aid and hide the felonious couple.

With the WHIP organization looking for them in the Portland Metro area, they now were alerted that Paul and Cara had slipped through their hands. Everyone now knew to focus on the Oregon Coast to find Paul and Cara. What they didn't know was that the reports of the blood trail, and discharged firearm, did confirm one was wounded; but they would find no hospital or doctor report of a patient being treated for a gunshot wound.

All local hospitals and doctors received requests to advise law enforcement if they had anyone matching the description. Joy was a mother, grandmother, and simply the kindest heart that anyone could ever imagine. But it was easy to understand why she was named "Julie". She took them both in and they had a chance to hide, heal, and plan what the heck to do next. Interestingly, the big headline in one of the newspapers from the Salem and Portland area provided the following story.

Portland: *An inmate at the Multnomah County Jailhouse, identified as a known "Master-at-Arms" for a local notorious gang was involved in providing information to the Portland Police Bureau; the information lead to the discovery of multiple edged weapons that were to be used to break-out and escape. The escape plot was foiled, when (name omitted pending investigation) assisted jail staff to locate the hidden weapons; most certainly saving many staff lives.*

The inmate was then placed in Protective Custody to ensure his safety; the repercussions of the outlaw gangsters was to place a contract on the previous member in retaliation. The plot was to act in the evening, when shift levels were at a minimum. A visitor had apparently introduced an item that could unlock the cell door – which would then free an inmate to overtake and kill an Officer, they would then cascade failure the cell block – creating an armed riot to overcome all authorities in the building; one floor at a time.

It is expected that the informant will be transferred to the Oregon DOC Administrative Segregation (Protective Custody) Unit in the near future. He will be provided an opportunity to testify via the internet connectivity of the facility when the trial begins. A dozen inmates in the jail were found with the weapons hidden in their cells; however, officials are not discussing details of the investigation at this time. A spokesperson for the facility advised that they had suspicions and a covert investigation was already underway – but the confirmation information provided by the previous gang member provided clues as to the location of the created weapons.

Interestingly, within a week, Paul and Cara read that the previous gang member that had been transferred successfully to the ADSEG for Protective Custody was only there a week; when he called for assistance and held the legs up of a cellmate that was attempting to commit suicide. The Officers responded, called for a medical response, and because of the alert by the ex-gang member…they were able to save the life of an Adult in Custody, (AIC). The facility Superintendent provided a personal letter of thanks to the lifesaving, compliant, chapel-going, religious, ex-gang member!

It was a magical transformation; the man was a leper of crime, and yet he had been reborn unto a life dedicated to helping his neighbor. It was perhaps almost Biblical, and yet the newspaper took a spin on how dangerous a criminal past he had, his association with the underbelly of crime; and how he was perhaps escaping justice until his court date. It was fortunate that the Oregon Department of Corrections utilized an adaptive and flexible process that was dependent upon each individual; the "Oregon Accountability Model" would allow for the transformation to be positive. Once incarcerated in the facilities, the man could have an opportunity to prove himself worthy of a second chance.

Paul was no judge of man; but honestly, he thought that the rules for using The Healing would have prevented him from using it to bring this thug back to life. Rule number two, (that he had personally adapted, was "no bad or evil") would have been a hurdle for this character. Paul probably regretted saving the young man's life for about a week, but now he was rejoicing in the good behavior, changed attitude, and stepping out of the gang mentality.

Because most gang cultures require, "Blood in – Blood out" it meant that to try and leave or step out of the gang would mean there was an automatic trigger pull on a member getting to the reborn man in ADSEG. If any member of the gang, (or anyone wanting to join the unauthorized organization) could put their hands on him and hurt or kill; they would have completed the task necessary for membership, (referred to as "Earning their Bones".)

This previously dangerous offender was the focus of multiple illegal gangs trying to hurt or kill him; even within the Protective Custody Unit. There were several gang members hiding out in the protective custody unit, if one wanted to regain status, and rejoin the gang, they too – would want to take advantage of being in the unit to hit the target.

Paul and Cara both believed that this newly re-born man would rather sacrifice himself, than to hurt or kill anyone else ever again. They both also believed that the media had proven itself not to be trusted to report the truth. Newspapers would print what TV's said and vice-versa. Paul believed at least he was too far away to influence anyone's opinion one way or another on the matter of the Adult in Custody.

While the previous gang member had a notorious past, (and would be held accountable by the law) he was no longer a threat to anyone. The only threats were all around him; he was a sheep in a wolf den, thank goodness the Oregon staff could not be corrupted, ensuring the safety of the young man; until court at least.

Paul and Cara would watch and try to track the fish out of water; Cara was healing internally as well as her back now was regaining color. Julie kept the two in home-cooked meals to heal and rest. Paul hadn't told Cara the pain he felt when he had saved her…it was tougher on him than usual. He wouldn't dare say anything to his lover, but he found out that strangers were different than the direct loved ones. He loved Cara deeply, he had to do it without even thinking or considering any consequences. Half the time, Paul didn't know what the use of his gift would bring upon him anyway.

Because of his love for Cara, or the severity of the wound, (or whatever God had chosen as a factor) Paul found himself collapsed after saving her life. If it wasn't for Julie coming to pick them up and shelter them, they both may have died. She was surely a God-send to them at the right time; and her faith and friendship of Cara would never end. She was unwavering and after all this time, she was able to keep a secret from the community as well as law enforcement. These everyday "angels" that came to Paul or Cara – were faultless and courageous!

Paul and Cara were almost relaxing enough to let their guard down, Julie made it easy. The couple decided it was best not to watch the news, the wildfire rumors and accusations against the couple continued to escalate, (one report tied them to terrorists) and the public was being "spoon-fed" lies and falsehoods. It was too disheartening for the two to endure watching the Communist Bastards!

Cara was collecting newspaper articles, to create a scrapbook; but now she burned all the lies and hate that had been spread publicly and falsely; not wanting to even ask Julie about picking up newspapers for information. They were now going to ignore, rather than read, all the disinformation. Cara was very hurt that they would spread lies about her; but she was infuriated that they were publicly attacking Paul, (and even the business that he and Dick had started together.) The young lovers wondered if anyone in the public would ever believe the **truth** – or if they would die somehow and never be able to tell their side of the story. She knew the records and history would reflect the lies and falsehoods; it would probably become even more impossible to reveal the truth – as more time passed.

Cara was determined to write something down; some reality to the bull-crap that was being flung onto the barn door, (if you threw enough – some will stick!) so she began from the start and began to update and keep a journal. In this way, at least she could be able to say, "THIS is what really happened – you Fake-News bastards!" She decided not to tell Paul, since he may not want her to keep anything that might tie or associate her with him. Cara felt like *Patty Hearst*, for crying out loud. She just wanted something that she could write that would tell the true story from her point of view and actually living the crazy roller-coaster. She would be hindered by the newspaper clippings, the public would read, "the story" but Cara would record the event. She would not do so, without Paul approving and providing the background when he was solo. The culmination of the recording of the events, would at least prove interesting to parents of the two victims of society. In this manner, Cara believed they would not go down without a fight; (even if the fight would come posthumously.)

Julie was covertly in contact with Seneca and Paul's family, (primarily through Paul's Uncle Don) gathering resources and funding to help hide the desperados. Paul's plan included touching base with his partner, (Dick Spencer) to sign a power of attorney; allowing Dick to sell or buy Paul's half of the business. Paul and Cara were certain they could never live freely in the old community; they would need funds to find and buy a new location, to build a life together. Paul secretly would love to be what he was to begin with; a vet in a small town that appreciates him. Cara and he could perhaps do this; (with a prerequisite that they change their names – and Paul wear his gloves when treating.)

It was the unspoken wish for the future; but it was all the two lovers could do to hold it together – hope, would be their future. Paul had the utmost faith in Dick, he had saved his life, given him a second chance; he would be fair in the settlement of the business. Paul wouldn't even give the notion a second thought. Most businessmen would love to say, "I saved my only partner's life, he kind of owes me!" It was in a very real sense, a blood oath that Dick would be honored to fulfill. He was living his life large, savoring each and every day that he normally would not have with them.

Dick Spencer was acting strangely, he was whistling at work…and he had this wonderful and inviting smile that never seem to leave him. He began to keep a small calendar that he was putting "gold stars" on dates that he saved an animal life. Calendars were covered with kitties and puppies' stars. His motto that he would be heard saying repeatedly, "Every day is a holiday, and every meal is a banquet!"

Dick assumed Paul's role in the cat shelter, taking one day a week to treat, examine, or just laugh at the stray or feral cats. Now and then, he would hide a small ball of catnip in the sweater pocket of the new – "old lady" that took care of the house full of cats.

Chapter 21

Julie received a strange letter in the mail, postmarked from nearby Charleston, when opened, the letter began with a salutation, "Dear Friend Flicka," Paul recognized the typed letter from Dr. Grey. Paul wondered if he was being taunted by the arm of WHIP, it was an obvious sign that everyone was in danger; Grey knew where they were! The letter made empty promises of not holding him in any way or inducing coma; but Paul knew better. Grey was not to be trusted. Paul was surprised a warning came at all, he expected a flash-bang grenade, or maybe a gas grenade, but an actual letter asking to meet him; this felt different.

Paul began to wonder if the ancient proverb could be correct; "The enemy of my enemy – is my friend?" He began to wonder what might happen if he took control of this situation; instead of just letting it happen to them, or someone springing a trap on them. Paul liked that idea better than the past interactions. He knew he could depend upon Julie, she was trustworthy and loyal. Paul had a friend similar to Julie, he spoke to Cara about his buddy, Allen New.

Allen had worked with the boats in the harbor, (near the Veterinarian Clinic) and had Paul remove a few hooks from him now and then at the charge of a cleaned fish. Sometimes he may cut his finger or hand – so that too, was on the menu. It didn't happen often, but anytime Paul was needed; he helped his buddy, Allen. Paul knew he could depend upon New!

With the culmination of Allen and Julie, Paul and Cara put their heads together, they would mold these bastards into the target, and then shoot them, like clay pigeons at the Seneca Shooting Range! The shoe would be on the other foot, Paul and Cara would have a plan that included back-up's too. The first step was to use a wrist rocket to shoot a note in a rock right through Corrie's window. Paul wanted to do it, but Cara wouldn't have it! "No, that bastard," she smiled, "shot me, and if all I get for retribution is tossing a rock through a window…I'm going to be the one that does it!"

It was a sticky and calm midnight, with no visible moon to guide a shot in the dark. Paul was driving, and Cara was the hit-woman! As the vehicle came to a halt, (as close as they dared) two dark figures exited the vehicle, no courtesy light was on, doors were squished close by the two butts. Paul led the way, although he wasn't positive in the directions in the dark. Soon, they could see the faint glow of the gilded cage they had been held previously. Cara got into position, as Paul handed her a small stone to rubber-band the note they had prepared. Cara's smile and teeth were all that Paul could see – until she pulled out a pair of steel ball-bearings! Paul may have motioned, "No!" but Cara launched the first steely message; it flew like an eagle, striking a large picture window that must have cost a fortune! She quickly reloaded and sent the message to Corrie, "Cara had balls of steel!" The two took off immediately, only lights and alarms that were left to cry alone, filling the night. The young lovers jumped into the awaiting vehicle and Paul sped off, after delivering the message to the man that shot his future wife! Paul hoped it would resonate, breathe a bit, and then kick like a jackass into motion; "The game was afoot!"

A similar response was sent to "Grey's gotta pay!" via the mail to the Charleston address that they had found on the letter. Cara's new pet name for Dr. Grey, seem to stick, like his horseshit on the barn door. From that point forward, he was referred to as, "Grey's gotta pay!" The two lovers would laugh together; it seemed like a long time had passed since they laughed together. For a third or tertiary plan, Paul made personal contact with a friend of his that just might be counted on, in a pinch. Paul hoped he could count on her, but she was the only other female Paul knew that had balls of steel. She would either help or hinder, time would tell.

The date with destiny was set, the following day Paul and Cara were preparing to drive to Horsfall Beach, (it was a right before the big bridge) there was a special handicap ramp made for anyone to see the beautiful beach that stretches for miles, before the bay. The perfectly sloped ramp would snake up the side of the sand dunes from the parking lot. Allowing any tourist to simply park, walk on the sidewalk to the ramp, and walk to see a breathtaking view – without getting one sand grain in their shoe!

The intent would be to monitor the arrival from the high point advantage overlooking the parking lot, observe Corrie and his clan coming, as well as Dr. Grey's gotta pay; it would put the ocean at their back. Cara wasn't quite sure she was comfortable, but when Paul explained his logic, it seemed reasonable. The part of the invite that dictated, "No weapons" would be disregarded, and Paul and Cara were expecting it. There were numerous reasons to realize there was no honor among these spirit-thieves! They stood behind money and power, the two things that corrupt absolutely. They were about to get a dose of Oregonian size ten, right in their ass!

Paul and Cara enjoyed arriving an hour early to watch for the soul-thieves people trying to blend in, but looking particularly out of place, on the Oregon Coast. Paul and Cara had no weapon to shoot the blood-thieves, but they were determined not to shed blood. Paul prepared a few things, playing in the sand and beach, (perhaps for the last time.) Cara kept a keen watch, seeing and identifying tourists arriving much too fast in the open parking lot – then speeding off after a photo or selfie.

The speed limit to get to the park was strictly enforced by the God-made speed bumps that have twisted, buckled, and erupted from the blacktop; only the newly leveled parking area and staging area for horseback riding on the beach is nice – the trip to get there was slowly navigating the crippled blacktop.

Paul and Cara enjoyed a small sandwich, bottled water, and shared a bag of chips. They never would have guessed the black SUV's arriving would be the party-pooper thieves, they anticipated – but of course when the two groups set eyes on each other; time just stopped. Paul and Cara wanted to yell from their high ground advantage, "Corrie, meet Dr. Grey!"

Paul halfway anticipated gunfire or at least weapons drawn at this point, but no one violated the weapons rule, yet. They didn't exactly shake hands, but they both probably figured to obtain the objective, and then decide where to go next. Paul and Cara were the target, not an opposing force. Grey and Money both must have decided to approach this like businessmen, but Paul would wait to see if they were going to behave like gentlemen.

The goons left their gooney-birds at the bottom of the ramp, posted and trying to hide weapons that were probably inside their jackets – that they wore to the coast. As the two powerbrokers approached upward from the ramp, Paul motioned Cara and then raised his arm and warned the two to stop, within speaking range, (or at least yelling range.) Cara stood behind Paul, not carrying anything, but acting like she was armed…with a fake air pistol that looked authentic. She would brandish it if a little flash of the weapon would cast a little doubt in the bastards.

"We just want to let you know we're sorry about how we first approached this," the doctor began, "it was apprehensible, and we want to ensure you, it won't ever happen again!"

"I'm sure you know that our organization," Corrie began, "has never physically hurt you, robbed you of DNA, or even taken your blood."

"You only drug, abduct, kidnap, and shoot my fiancé," Paul quickly responded. "You both need to know that we don't choose one of you to befriend and cooperate – we choose neither of you!" The two fugitives stood, knowing that the lies spread about them, would never let them live free – as they were before, anyway. "We are working with an organization that is comparable with you two, that has reached out to us – asking, not telling, and they will hide us out from you and your kind," Paul advised loudly.

Today, the two nemeses would have to accept the no vote, especially when Cara flashed the weapon for just a little peek. It was just the right touch, to reach out and say, "Hi, our handgun is closer than your goon and guns!" It sent a slight reminder to the two that Cara and Paul were not to be toyed with today. Cara looked at Corrie and simply said, "I owe you one bullet, bastard – just give me a reason to pop your head like a melon!"

Paul took the center stage and advised the two, "Here is what's going to happen, you two need to back the hell off of us, stop spreading your propaganda and lies, we are going to go with door number three, and you two may receive a conciliation prize – shared research and data from our benefactor." "Everyone wins, nobody gets perforated, and we all work together; for the good of mankind – not for power or money!" Paul smiled as he dropped two small business cards from his hand, one for each of them.

That was the signal for Cara to take the leap, just like an Oregon Duck or OSU Beaver, the two jumped over the edge of the overlook! The sand below would catch them, but there was some debris that required maneuvering. The two businessmen weren't sure what to do, or expect, so each scrambled for a card, they stood pointing at the beach and ocean that was on the other side of the huge sand dune.

The goonies ran in their Italian shoes into the sand dune path, that the public had made in sandals or Oregonian bare feet. Sand consumed their shoes and ankles, making it difficult to trudge forward. It was at least five minutes before they could even reach the top of the dune, below them was three football fields of space before the ocean. Even a marksman shot for a handgun in the hands of a Navy Seal, Paul and Cara were headed out to sea! The two were moving like otters, until they grabbed something that seemed to be propelling them.

The military veteran, Allen New was heading out to sea, pulling the longest damn pair of ski ropes the two had ever grabbed onto! The ocean was cool, but the wet suits underneath kept them warm. They simply held on and clipped onto a harness to drag them on their boogie boards. The two lovers laughing all the way!

Goonies stupidly fired a few pot shots toward the boat, (that was out of range) as they attempted to run down an Oregon Coast sand dune. Not sure if they should be shooting anyway, (because the idiots could get lucky and kill the non-expendable target) they ceased fire when they got to the level, flat, sand. As they began to try and holster their weapons, in an effort to hide their recent discharging stupidity; they looked down the beach only to see something they hadn't expected.

The female Sheriff and her deputies were storming the beach, brandishing their own weapons on horseback! The law enforcement posse was yelling, "GET DOWN – ON THE GROUND!" The Sheriff was leading the charge and the horses were on the idiots in no time! She met the first goon and grabbed his hair, pounded him against her gelding and saddle, it bounced him to the ground with more force than may have been needed. The rest of the pack simply hit the sand in their *Gucci* and *Armani*'s!

The Coos County Mounted Posse had sprung into action; they had encircled the parking lot, on horseback. They were closing in on everyone wanting to drive away from the scene. A few horses and the Posse with weapons slowed everyone down to a snail race. The entire thing was orchestrated like some well-trained dance choreography.

Discharging a firearm on the beach, alleged kidnapping and extortion, and other pertinent charges may be filed – or dropped, but it called for the booking into the Coquille Jailhouse for the weekend. It would probably give a good vet and his assistant and opportunity to get far away from these lying, life-thieves.

Chapter 22

The New boat ride led the duo to an easy release of the rope and a glide to the beach. They had some clothing all wadded up, allowing them to change and mix into the public with no sign of the events, except the wet hair. Cara turned the corner, following Paul to a designated spot to be picked up. They would then sign some forms with Dick, giving him the power of attorney to sell Paul's half of the business.

Dick smiled at the couple as he pulled up. They both got in the back seat, and the car whisked them off to a better future. Dick began to talk while keeping his eye on the road, "Cara, you know the practice really can't get along without you, so I'm afraid we can't let you go at this time." He seemed to have a straight face, and he was the one that had hired Cara to begin with; but, Cara couldn't believe he would be so heartless, or fail to understand she couldn't remain in the area without Paul, nor would she remain at the office.

Cara knew the stupidity of the idea would set Paul afire; so, she simply said, "I don't think Paul would agree with that idea." Cara looked into Paul's eyes and knew that she would always find loving support, all she could see is the adoration Paul had for Cara. He didn't even blink or smile.

"I think until Cara finishes what she started at work," Paul agreed, "she probably would need to be at work…since you're the boss and all now, Dick."

Cara's heart sank into her feet – these two men must be bigger fools than she thought, "If that's what they both think of me…just an employee!" she began to fume.

Dick pulled the vehicle over to the side of the road; reaching back to look directly at the two fugitives in the back seat, "You are not done with the Clinic, until you finish what you started…Paul can't live without you, will you do the honor and marry him?" Dick opened the small box in his hand with a flick of a thumb, the brilliant ring had a couple carat diamond – shaped like a heart!

Cara began to cry...she kissed Paul as her hand went up and grabbed the box from Dick's hand with the force she could wield on Dr. Grey! She stopped kissing long enough to squeal out a "yes," the two would be inseparable after that. It was a golden day, it was a diamond day, it was truly a day of days! Paul handed Cara a small business card, it had an old tree with many branches embossed, the name on the card was simply, "Arthur". There were Celtic knots circling the tree, and under Arthur's name was simply, "Order of Angelic Knights – O.A.K.".

Paul promised to Cara, "These are the people and the organization that will never harm us, they will hide us from those that would do us harm," Paul put his hand to his heart – "I promise they are different, they will cherish us both." Paul explained, "They are well funded, but they have no pride, no agenda, no need to lie, they are our wondrous and gentle hosts." Paul took her hand, "I know it's hard to place your trust in anyone after all we've been through," he stared into her eyes, "I place my life and yours into their hands, fully trusting them – you should too."

Cara knew that Paul wouldn't lie to her, and she knew that if he promised all this, it must be true. But she had a little doubt, because of the terrible past that the two had endured; she said, "I have only one question Paul," she hesitated, "how do you know that you're not misplacing faith in this – OAK?"

Paul pulled a picture from his back pocket, it was a picture of him with his brother, "Lance is my brother, he is known to hundreds of Angels, as..." Arthur". This is his organization, he is at least the head of it, we can trust him!"

Cara nodded positively, kissed Paul, and motioned forward, telling her boss, "Move it Dick!" Dick smiled and pulled the car into gear as they cruised toward someplace in Vermont. The public would never know all the events and chronological story of Paul and Cara, if it weren't for Cara keeping her journal, filling in the pieces of Paul's adverse adventures too. She kept it for a year, she then forwarded it to the writer of this novel to awaken the world to something they hadn't seen, felt, or experienced lately...HOPE.

The money removed the website, the power crushed the truth, but there was one thing that remained that someone couldn't cover up, couldn't deal with, and they had names!

From the burn unit –

Malcolm: A beautiful black child that now had hair!

Amy: A beautiful oriental that can run and walk again!

Charles: A beautiful kid that could see – everything!

Delores: A two-year-old – that had all four limbs!

Paul: A young man whose chest could hold a lover!

Charity: A small girl that would be beautiful!

What the rest of the world would not know…until later; each individual that was touched by an Angel, would reflect no sign of sterility. Each of them over the next year – also saved someone else's life! It was the, "after-blessing" that would place each and every one into a position to save some other person's life. It was a wonderful gift that kept giving!

Cara gave birth to a baby girl and a baby boy; but no one ever sent any announcements, they relocated successfully, pulling Paul along with them, wherever they went.

Not The End?

Epilogue

These were the chronicles of Paul that Cara handed down, capturing some of their misadventures, and some of the people Paul influenced. If not captured somehow by their first-hand observation, the true adventures would be lost in obscurity. Neither Money or Power corrupted Paul and Cara; they remained true to the target of anonymity. Their names were changed to protect the family they had made, after the spreading of both – the Bird Fire, and The Healing.

The Healing of the children in the burn unit, became known as the, "Hospital Terrorist Abduction" and the children have been removed from the rosters and all documentation destroyed.

The years that followed…resulted in many healed being captured, sedated, studied, and eventually the result of an autopsy somewhere.

But those that were not captured…were healthy, lively, and fertile!

About the Author

Growing up in Eastern Oregon, Sonny Rider saw a few folks that had missing or maimed body parts from working in the wood mills. His own father had his arm pulled into a planer. This was the motivation that moved him into the military in 1976 (close of Vietnam War era). After Naval Cryptologic school, he spent his first year in Iceland, (wondering why they ignored his California request.)

After serving in Scotland for several years, (and meeting his wife) college followed; and then after another few years aboard the USS Enterprise (CVN-65); he served thirty years for the Oregon Department of Corrections. He played taps as a retired, Honor Guard Bugler twice in two weeks this year.

Authoring books to inspire others, you may also enjoy: The Finding and also The Finding of Angels, by Sonny Rider. Thank you – and God Bless.

Made in the USA
San Bernardino, CA
08 March 2019